Figures in Orbits of Symphony
Stories and Ideas

Angelyn Spignesi Kopylec Arden

En Route Books and Media, LLC
Saint Louis, MO

Make the time

En Route Books and Media, LLC

5705 Rhodes Avenue

St. Louis, MO 63109

contactus@enroutebooksandmedia.com

Cover credit: Sebastian Mahfood from Artwork by Author, Markers on Canvas

© 2022 Angelyn Spignesi Kopylec Arden

ISBN-13: 978-1-956715-67-5

Library of Congress Control Number: 2022941878

TABLE OF CONTENTS

IDEAS

STORIES

IDEAS

IDEAS

Figures of the Psyche in Orbits of Symphony: The "Space between" Spirit and Matter as a Complete Interactive Circuit[1]

From my study of and work in the psyche for the last four decades, and ten books, I have learned about psychological figures, and how, working with them carefully, can be a way not only to self-knowledge, but also healing and growth to one's true vocation knowing oneself and others. These figures are not spirit or matter but communicate spirit through matter and live in matter symbolizing its connection to spirit. I have called the "space" from where these figures come, metaxy, following Plato and Simone Weil.[2]

However, "space" and "between" are misnomers since, as I have written:

My work does not uphold the (neo)Platonic denigration of matter yet, in a phenomenological manner, sees the divine working in and through matter, circulating. Therefore, to say that this is an intermediate or middle

---

[1] An earlier version of this paper was delivered, on November 20, 2021, to the Connecticut Association for Jungian Psychology.

[2] See my article "Metaxy, Forms, and Healing: A Neoplatonic-Augustinian Approach to the Integration of Depth Psychology and Christianity" forthcoming in *Integratus* 1, (2023).

realm is a misnomer. These figures are not *between* yet move in a circuit communicating the divine to human and vice versa, without negating their difference. [3]

I use this term, metaxy, as others might use "mundus imaginalis" or "imaginal" or "soul" or "world soul", however, there are confusions with the use of those other terms. For example, Henri Corbin, the originator of the term "mundus imaginalis", disagrees with how it is used as "imaginal" in not taking enough from the philosophical transcendentals which "'necessitate them and legitimize them'". [4] The word "soul" has become a mishmash of meanings from many cultures and newer opinions.

Though it also can be seen to be between Matter and Spirit, "unconscious" also has been a term quite misused and misunderstood. Metaxy is not beneath the concrete and material, yet around it. A person's personal unconscious is of metaxy as is the collective unconscious. As I have elaborated upon and exemplified in my previous work, figures of metaxy move between Spirit and Matter in a circuit. I will discuss how some are more aligned with the Spirit, some with the Matter.

---

[3] My "Metaxy, Forms, and Healing" above, 9. Also, see my *Orbits of Symphony* (Denver, Colorado: Outskirts Press, 2015).

[4] Tom Cheetam, *All the World an Icon: Henry Corbin and the Angelic Function of Beings* (Berkeley, California: North Atlantic Books, 2012), 32-33.

I also think that the word "archetype" has accumulated a multitude of meanings since Jung first used it in his work. I did not use it, for that reason, in my article on metaxy. Plato originally used the word, stemming from the Greek root *arch* meaning preeminent, to describe forms that are transcendent, independent of material particularities, histories, and cultures. Jung used it as unconscious patterns, or "*regularly recurring modes of apprehension*",[5] which lead to an image at one end and instinct at the other: the image triggers and gives direction to instinct through unconscious apprehension.[6]

Jung thought that archetypes made up the collective unconscious, apart from personal contents, that is made up of "the psychic life of our ancestors right back to the earliest beginnings. It is the matrix of all conscious psychic occur-

---

[5] C. G. Jung, "Instinct and the Unconscious," in *The Structure and Dynamics of the Psyche*, 2nd ed., vol. 8 of *The Collected Works of C. G. Jung*, ed. William McGuire, Sir Herbert Read, Michael Fordham, and Gerhard Adler, trans. R. F. C. Hull, Bollingen Series XX (Princeton, NJ: Princeton University Press, 1978), 137-8, his italics (I will use page numbers, not paragraph numbers, for Jung's Collected Works which I will abbreviate as *CW*).

[6] Jung, "Instinct and the Unconscious,"136-8, and see C.G. Jung, *The Archetypes and the Collective Unconscious*, 2nd ed., vol. 9, part I of *CW*, ed. William McGuire, Sir Herbert Read, Michael Fordham, and Gerhard Adler, trans. R. F. C. Hull, Bollingen Series XX (Princeton, NJ: Princeton University Press, 1980).

rences, and hence it exerts an influence that compromises the freedom of consciousness in the highest degree, since it is continually striving to lead all conscious processes back into the old paths."[7] Though he says it stems from Plato and Augustine, he uses it not as transcendental but as "accumulated, life-experiences" and "not a question of 'representations'".[8] These accumulated life-experiences are "engraved on the human mind, helping it to form its judgments." [9]

---

[7] C.G. Jung, "Constitution and Heredity in Psychology," in *The Structure and Dynamics of the Psyche*, 2nd ed., vol. 8 of *CW*, 112.

[8] C.G. Jung, "On the Nature of the Psyche," in *The Structure and Dynamics of the Psyche*, 2nd ed., vol. 8 of *CW*, 165. See also C.G. Jung, "Analytical Psychology and the 'Weltanschauung'" in *The Structure and Dynamics of the Psyche*, 2nd ed., vol. 8 of *CW*, 376: Archetypes make up the collective unconscious which is "the mighty deposit of ancestral experience accumulated over millions of years, the echo of prehistoric happenings to which each century adds an infinitesimally small amount of variation and differentiation. Because the collective unconscious is, in the last analysis a deposit of world-processes embedded in the structure of the brain and the sympathetic nervous system, it constitutes in its totality a sort of timeless and eternal world-image which counterbalances our conscious, momentary picture of the world."

[9] Jung's reference to Herbert of Cherbury, "Instinct and the Unconscious," 136.

James Hillman's work uses the term "archetype" retaining more of its original Platonic and neo-Platonic sense, though not as transcendental or relating to Forms that are transcendental, thereby not discussing the relation of archetypes to virtues.[10] His work establishes convincingly the reality of the "*tertium*" between matter and spirit, in his terminology, the soul, which is composed of archetypes.[11] I prefer to return to the Neoplatonic study of figures of metaxy which allows access to Forms, and also to humans, and a way spirit is circulating in matter through such figures.

I see that Forms are transcendental, including virtues.[12] They become more embodied as they move through figures which then have a direct impact on our ideas, emotions, desires, impulses, actions, and are seen in stories and myths throughout history. "Members", as discussed in my *Orbits of Symphony*, are parts of our psyche associated with members in our family and inform our understanding of Forms.

---

[10]James Hillman, *Re-Visioning Psychology* (NY, NY: Harper Colophon, 1977); *Archetypal Psychology: A Brief Account* (Dallas, Texas: Spring Publications, 1985), and his other works selected in *A Blue Fire* (NY, NY: Harper and Row, 1989).

[11] I am grateful for Hillman's teachings on the crucial reality of the figures of the psyche as well as the importance of staying precisely close to the image and not leaving that to go to a conceptual overlay.

[12] See my "Metaxy, Forms, and Healing" and *Orbits of Symphony* (Denver, CO: 2015).

In their embodiment, their way of incarnating, Forms present us with figures and each figure comes with a constellation, with a story involving other figures. It is never just one, it is never, for example, the trickster or the lover or the king or maiden, each is embedded in a constellation, a story, folktale, or myth, that gives us the archetype. So when I discuss figures I am referring to each as within a constellation.[13]

So Forms inform through figures, and each is in a constellation of events, affects, attitudes and behaviors that can cross generations and become archetypes, stories and myths of a culture. Figures that apply particularly to one's own family are called members.

Figures can be in metaxy yet not be relevant to everyone's purpose or authentic being, not part of everyone's soul. Figures and members making up one's personality, psychopathology, and vocation in life is the way soul moves in a person. In that way, one's soul, the way the figures in a

---

[13] I'm concerned that this sense of archetype has been altered by modern spiritual psychologies. Forms include patterns of behavior over centuries, yet such behavior is expressive of the transcendental world. In this way I differ from Jung's and Hillman's use of archetype which corresponds more exclusively to the former, to patterns of behaviors and experiences over generations.

lifetime animate a person, circulating between matter and spirit, is a part of metaxy.

We can perceive ourselves more deeply and comprehensively through the figures when we have self-awareness through the working of grace; when we lose self-awareness and its subsequent unifying potential, we can fall into a hole feeling sundered as if we are flowing out into the figures and dissolving into them. This can occur when figures are used defensively in will-to-power reactive responses.

As I have discussed in my work, some of the figures of metaxy are will-to-power responses to deep wounds and thereby correspond to how C. G. Jung saw "complexes". Jung found complexes while doing association tests in which he presented words to subjects and asked for their associations to them. He was measuring the speed of reactions to these words. He found that the process was interrupted when the subject paused and could not respond for an extended time or at all to certain words. He found these disturbances to be caused, as he describes, by "the autonomous behavior of the psyche, that is, by assimilation. It was then that I discovered the feeling-toned complexes, which had always been registered before as *failures to react*."[14]

---

[14]C. G. Jung, "A Review of the Complex Theory," in *The Structure and Dynamics of the Psyche,* 2nd ed., vol. 8 of *CW*, 93, his italics.

He further described this process as a constellation:

When we say that a person is "constellated" we mean that he has taken up a position from which he can be expected to react in a quite definite way. But the constellation is an automatic process which happens involuntarily and which no one can stop of his own accord. The constellated contents are definite complexes possessing their own specific energy... What happens in the association test also happens in every discussion between two people. In both cases there is an experimental situation which constellates complexes that assimilate the topic discussed or the situation as a whole, including the parties concerned. The discussion loses its objective character and its real purpose, since the constellated complexes frustrate the intentions of the speakers and may even put answers into their mouths which they can no longer remember afterwards.[15]

One can see the relation of complexes to how we understand addictions today. Jung continues:

Every constellation of a complex postulates a disturbed state of consciousness. The unity of consciousness is disrupted and the intentions for the will are impeded or made impossible. Even memory is often noticeably affected, as we have seen. The complex must therefore be a psychic factor which, in terms of energy, possesses a value that sometimes exceeds that of our conscious

---

[15] Jung, "A Review of the Complex Theory," 94-95.

intentions, otherwise such disruptions of the conscious order would not be possible at all. And in fact, an active complex puts us momentarily under a state of duress, of compulsive thinking and acting, for which under certain conditions the only appropriate term would be the judicial concept of diminished responsibility.[16]

Therefore, as I use the term, a figure of metaxy can be problematic in the way that Jung discusses here, and then it becomes a "complex". This is what I mean when I say that I see a figure of metaxy as a constellation. Each carries a relationship with other figures that affects how it presents itself, indeed its identity.

Jung and Hillman contributed much to our understanding of how figures are not made or invented by the conscious: they are found by it, to our advantage. They come to us and so it is possible for us to establish a relationship with them. I add: they are given to us by God to work out the deficiencies in power as well as the defenses against such throughout the family line, in order to cleanse and renew our soul, redeem it for ourselves and others.

Jung further discusses complexes:

Janet and Morton Prince both succeeded in producing four to five splittings of the personality, and it turned out that each fragment of personality had its own peculiar

---

[16] Jung, "A Review of the Complex Theory," 96.

character and its own separate memory. These fragments subsist relatively independently of one another and can take one another's place at any time, which means that each fragment possesses a high degree of autonomy. My findings in regard to complexes corroborate this somewhat disquieting picture of the possibilities of psychic disintegration, for fundamentally there is no difference in principle between a fragmentary personality and a complex[17]... Today we can take it as moderately certain that complexes are in fact "splinter psyches." The aetiology of their origin is frequently a so-called trauma, an emotional shock or some such thing, that splits off a bit of the psyche. Certainly, one of the commonest causes is a *moral conflict*, which ultimately derives from the apparent impossibility of affirming the whole of one's nature. This impossibility presupposes a direct split, no matter whether the conscious mind is aware of it or not[18]

Today we would no longer call trauma "so-called", yet it is clear empirically that trauma is the major source of splitting, and the first psychoanalysts were the ones who recognized that to various degrees. The splitting is not in the

---

[17]Jung, "A Review of the Complex Theory," p. 96-97; also, see my discussion of Prince's work in my *Orbits of Symphony*.

[18]Jung, "A Review of the Complex Theory," p. 98, italics mine. Also see C.G. Jung, "Psychological Factors in Human Behavior," in *The Structure and Dynamics of the Psyche*, 2nd ed., vol. 8 of *CW*, 121: "Complexes are psychic fragments which have split off owing to traumatic influences or certain incompatible tendencies."

psyche but a dissociation from the personal psyche, therefore "losing the soul" when one is caught in such a constellation of complexes. Note that his view of the cause is a moral conflict.[19]

Jung continues:

> Only when you have seen whole families destroyed by them [complexes], morally and physically, and the unexampled tragedy and hopeless misery that follow in their train, do you feel the full impact of the reality of the

---

[19]Jung's understanding of the numinosity of complexes gets to their relation to God, though, as an empiricist, he does not specifically go there—"It will no doubt be remembered what a storm of indignation was unleashed on all sides when Freud's works became generally known. This violent reaction of public complexes drove Freud into an isolation which has brought the charge of dogmatism upon him and his school. All psychological theoreticians in this field run the same risk, for they are playing with something that directly affects all that is uncontrolled in man – the *numinosum*, to use an apt expression of Rudolf Otto's. Where the realm of complexes begins the freedom of the ego comes to an end, for complexes are psychic agencies whose deepest nature is still unfathomed. Every time the researcher succeeds in advancing a little further towards the psychic *tremendum*, then, as before, reactions are let loose in the public, just as with patients who, for therapeutic reasons, are urged to take up arms against the inviolability of their complexes." Jung, "A Review of the Complex Theory," 103-104, italics his.

complexes. You then understand how idle and unscientific it is to think that a person can "imagine" a complex.[20]

I think of this impact of complexes as circuits within metaxy that resonate with mother, father, sister, and brother figures. That is, as the individual is born and develops, he/she is participating in particular Forms which resonate with accumulated problems and conflicts in the family and ancestry recapitulated in interpersonal relationships. I refer to this interaction as the circuit of metaxy. Each figure is given within a constellation with other members, all relating to gifts and psychopathologies handed down the family which are keys to pruning, purifying the individual to get to who he/she was made to be.

Therefore, my specific mother complex is part of the mother "archetype" but is individual to me: genetically, biologically, psychologically as handed down ancestrally and given as part of my (divinely ordained) vocation. How it is specific to me can be delineated by the term member. Familial and personal figures are members and *members* stream to *archetypes* (encompassing the particular pattern of the story of the members, their interactions, and that can appear in literature and myth) which stream to *Forms* which encompass that figure over time and space for many indivi-

---

[20]Jung, "A Review of the Complex Theory," p. 100-101.

duals across generations and cultures and are virtues.[21] Figures that have traumatized or hurt one deeply become the complex.

One only finds and can optimally work in one's vocation once the major complexes have been sorted through, processed, and integrated in one's psyche. That is the purging or burning the obstacles, given ancestrally by God, leading to becoming excellent vessels of the Spirit in communal giving to others.[22]

---

[21] I elaborate upon the distinction between members and Forms in *Orbits of Symphony*.

[22] See Jung on how only spirit can break conventions, and St. Paul: "Now it is necessary to have conventions; nothing would be more foolish than to destroy them. They would never have come to be if they were not really needed. And it is right to collapse before convention; we are meant to... To fight convention by futile arguments and attacks upon society only leads us into new convention worse than the one before. We really cannot circumvent it. The only thing that may break conventions is the spirit; it is worthwhile to break conventions for a new spirit. To oppose convention for a whim or a fad is nothing but foolish destruction if we succeed at all. But for the spirit it is something else. Spirit is constructive; out of spirit something can come, because it is a living thing and a fertilizing thing. So, naturally, it has a great advantage over mere conventions. Convention is never creative but spirit is always creative. You can find this psychology in the Epistles of St. Paul; everything that I am saying here he has

These complexes are based on trauma or disorders with the earliest members of one's family. This shows how split-off personalities, figures of our complexes, are related to personal histories.

But it is not only about one individual. Jung:

> We always find in the patient a conflict which at a certain point is connected with the great problems of society. Hence, when the analysis is pushed to this point, the apparently individual conflict of the patient is revealed as a universal conflict of his environment and epoch. Neurosis is thus nothing less than an individual attempt, however unsuccessful, to solve a universal problem; indeed it cannot be otherwise, for a general problem, a "question," is not an *ens per se*, but exists only in the hearts of individuals[23]... [This funnelling of the individual conflict into the general moral problem puts psychoanalysis far outside the confines of a merely medical therapy. It gives the patient a working philosophy of life based on empirical insights, which,

---

already said." C. G. Jung, *The Visions Seminars, Book One* (Zurich, Switzerland: Spring Publications, 1976), 165.

[23] C. G. Jung, "New Paths in Psychology," in *Two Essays on Analytical Psychology*, 2nd ed., vol. 7 of *The Collected Works of C. G. Jung*, eds. William McGuire, Sir Herbert Read, Michael Fordham, Gerhard Adler, trans. R. F. C. Hull, Bollingen Series XX (Princeton, NJ: Princeton University Press, 1977), p. 265, his italics.

besides affording him a knowledge of his own nature, also make it possible for him to fit himself into this scheme of things...][24]

The general moral problem at that time, as he states, was sexual morality. Now in the 21st century, it is how Spirit, and a spiritual life can be understood as foundational and the crux in a secular, materialistic, hyper-sexualized age. The other moral problem today is the mother/work woman question: how women can be mothers attuned to their children and also have a vocation outside that. This second moral problem is associated with the first: the necessity of a move to the feminine in the movement of society and religion to truly being virtuous.[25]

Finally, Jung concludes:

As can be seen, I have contented myself with describing only the essential features of the complex theory. I must refrain, however, from filling in this incomplete picture by a description of the problems arising out of the existence of autonomous complexes. Three important problems would have to be dealt with: the therapeutic, the philosophical, and the moral. All three still await discussion.[26]

---

[24] C. G. Jung, "New Paths in Psychology," 267

[25] In many ways, I see our culture as pre-Christian in its compulsive move to retaliation and materialism.

[26] C. G. Jung, "A Review of the Complex Theory," 104

In my view, Hillman and others have continued this work primarily in the therapeutic and philosophical[27] as I am continuing it through those as well as the moral. Jung appreciated this necessity though he did not comprehensively deal with it in his work except in specific places.

One place where Jung did include it:

We must read the Bible or we shall not understand psychology. Our psychology, our whole lives, our language and imagery are built upon the Bible. Again and again one comes across it in the unconscious of people who know practically nothing of it; yet these metaphors are in their dreams because they are in our blood.[28]

In my life, I have witnessed the Judeo-Christian heritage in the blood and how it can be used in therapeutic advances. As discussed, I have drawn from the neo-Platonic, Augustinian philosophical tradition in advancing such. This work thereby extends to the moral and theological issues as well as psychological, and therapeutic.

In my experience and study, I have learned how the moral problem is that one cannot explore metaxy without

---

[27] See James Hillman, *Re-Visioning Psychology*; *Archetypal Psychology: A Brief Account*; and his other works selected in *A Blue Fire*.

[28] C. G. Jung, *The Visions Seminars, Book One*, 156.

being connected to spirit, since the exploration of the realm between matter and spirit, often referred to as "unconscious", is a moral endeavor. There are varieties of figures and without the self-awareness that issues from consonance with spirit, one easily can fall asunder.

That is, first, one has to cleanse, purify oneself, to relate to and understand the figures of metaxy. There are positive and negative figures: some of the good and some of the bad or even evil. Some, particularly those figures that pertain to family members, have good and bad sides. If one engages in this area without self-awareness of one's own badness, without having worked on that, having it "burnt up", it would be easy to attract the bad and go under the "complexes" there. Thus, it would make it harder to see what is there and how we are being asked to know ourselves and others through it.

As I have explained, my mother figure is one part of mother "archetype" which includes many other ways of mothering. I say that my mother figure is a member (i.e., personal to me), and the mother archetype carries that in universal stories or myths that resonate with a Form (collective and metaphysical). Forms include virtues which are "higher" than familial members.

One has to cleanse to stay close to Christ and the Holy Spirit while engaging with the circuit of metaxy moving between spirit and matter. This includes self-possession and prayer, the cleanliness of oneself as a vessel. Here is an abstaining from evil in both deed and thought, attempting good works, while attempting in prayer and guidance to transform the evil within. Sorrow and suffering have to be acknowledged and accepted for transformative grace to annul the ancestral burdens and curses.

As I attempted such through the 80's, I engaged with metaxy and discovered figures there through a close textual and analytical reading of the novel *Jane Eyre*. That was only done while living a life very trimmed of worldly interests and pursuits, quite contemplative, and purposely focused on this exploration.

I then developed this work, bringing it to Christianity in my next eight books, as I worked in community and in the world. Since 1978, I have worked extensively on my dreams and those of others, as well as studying and writing on the psychology. Staying now for decades in dialogue with metaxy has led to an accessibility to the circuit flowing between figures and humans affecting personality, psychopathology, and relationships. This accessibility has developed to where I am able to see and hear images readily, and thus the short stories have emerged.[29] This process is not "automatic" yet, as I discuss in my metaxy article where I quoted authors speaking of their writing process,[30] I follow the images and

---

[29] See my *"Empty Nest" and Other Stories* (St. Louis, MO: Enroute Books and Media, 2022) as well as the stories in this book.

[30] See my "Metaxy, Forms, and Healing".

characters, and then I edit. Therefore, the stories are the culmination of my intellectual, emotional, and spiritual work.

Now I will recapitulate the findings of my work on the three figures of Reed, Brocklehurst, and Rochester. They are not members, my personal figures, though they emerged from the author Charlotte Brontë's members and, through her creativity and connection to spirit, these characters in her novel *Jane Eyre* streamed from Forms relevant to the population of the West, certainly, and beyond, now for over a century and seven decades, as they resonate with the figures in my personal life. I do think that Forms have "responsibility" for areas of populations and certain cultures. Perhaps Reed, Brocklehurst, and Rochester are imaged differently in Pacific Island cultures or others unlike that of the West, though *Jane Eyre* does have a very broad extension, and its films are seen worldwide.

Now to summarize and further discuss these three figures, I begin in the womb.

I have seen how the particular womb where you and I came to life is not an arbitrary place (Matthew 10:30, Psalm 139:13-16, Jeremiah 1:5, Exodus 4:11): our particular mother is immensely significant – how she received news about her fetus, her feeling about the pregnancy and previous pregnancies, her adjustments to hormonal and bodily changes – all these details are different for each mother and each birth, and they very much affect the way the baby comes to life, grows, and learns to love.

Anyone who looks at an infant can see the light of God emanating through. Mother and father then have to face that light daily, hourly, and thereby are forced to see their distance from it. Each reacts to seeing that distance from the light of God very differently.

Each mother is responsible for the infant's life or death in the womb and beyond, and the infant thereby senses her as omniscient, omnipotent – as having divine authority in the way she can stop or promote his or her life. The way the mother's womb, and she herself, is so easily identified as the Creator leads to idolatry of her and rebellion from her. This idolatry/rebellion is the source of the mother's power, her use or misuse of that power and, importantly, the misogyny of thousands of years.

The ideal would be courses on mothering and fathering for one to understand the ability of being seen by the infant at first as divine and to understand the necessity of what will be a rupture from one as seen as divine, one's role in this rupture and together move the child consciously through that.

But instead, as the child leaves, separates from the mother and father, even by speaking to others, walking, the "terrible twos" by saying "no", then going to school, having friends and loving others outside the family, and so forth, reconstitutes times the parents or caregivers were abandoned or betrayed or hurt and so they clutch or repel the child in response. These are will-to-power reactions to defend against their own emptiness and fear. This is when the parent is not emotionally attuned or available; these reactions of attacking or cutting off, mostly are repetitions of what the parents had experienced in childhood when they tried to separate. They can lead to trauma in their child who develops self-soothing behaviors to adapt to and deal with the stress – that is, the child seeks temporary pleasure, relief, and persists in such despite negative consequences. Here is the source of power patterns as well as addictions and, from my writing, since 1980, I have described three will-to-power figures in the psyche.[31]

I discovered and worked on these figures while first writing a book on eating disorders and then doing a close textual analysis on one third of the novel *Jane Eyre*.[32] Because the figures have spoken to and resonated with diverse populations for centuries, they also can be seen as "archetypes" resonating with Forms, but not being identical with Forms since the figures include the accumulation of indivi-

---

[31] The preceding section comes from my *The Articulate Silence of God* (Bloomington, Indiana: Xlibris, 2002).

[32] Angelyn Spignesi, *Starving Women: A Psychology of Anorexia Nervosa* (Dallas, Texas: Spring Publications, 1983); Angelyn Spignesi, *Lyrical-Analysis: The Unconscious through Jane Eyre* (Wilmette, Illinois: Chiron Publ., 1990).

dual histories and experience, Brontë's and our own. The Forms are metaphysically transcending generations informing the accumulation of individual histories. This understanding has led to my understanding of the "space" between the celestial and terrestrial, or, better put, when and how they contact one another.

As I discussed, in *Lyrical-Analysis: The Unconscious through Jane Eyre*, the fact that a novel that Charlotte Brontë wrote, in 1847, has characters that speak to populations since then, representing "universal" themes, shows that they point to Forms that are metaphysical. Classics are classics because the characters resonate with figures in the circuit, where God communicates to humans. Those that lead to virtues, as they do in *Jane Eyre*, sound right, they resonate with the music of the Forms of true reality. They lead us to a moment where truth is goodness is beauty and can be contemplated as such.[33]

There are certain ways to understand repetitive patterns that are passed down ancestrally (in one's biology, in one's upbringing) which are felt as one's destiny. Unattended ancestral burdens become defenses, sins, and a will-to-power that can destroy. These are both historically and spiritually motivated, and encompass our vocation given by God.

---

[33] See my discussion of these statements in my *Orbits of Symphony*.

Such burdens can be seen in light of these three figures: Reed, Brocklehurst, and Rochester. Each are defenses, ways to escape from how Spirit is working through one's body and one's life to prepare on for who one is in one's true vocation. To attend to them, dialogue with them, and understand the meaning in their affects is a huge task since the tendency is to identify with them or repress them which leads to being possessed by them, as Jung described above, and thereby thrown into a territory of sin and despair, a place that is truly cacophonous and disorienting. To suffer and work through them is to increase consonant space in oneself lending oneself closer to one's counterpart in the celestial world in Christ.

As I described them in *The Articulate Silence of God*:

John Reed is a pubescent, rebellious boy indulged by his mother. He overeats and is flabby, tyrannical, and continually tormenting of anyone who becomes his victim, until his cruelty turns on himself. Brocklehurst is a hypocritical clergyman who runs an orphanage (of which his mother was benefactress) for poor and neglected orphans. He preaches a God of fire and brimstone, and is arrogant, elitist, and dominating. He compares and contrasts as he "unconsciously" spreads filth and disease. Rochester is a wealthy landowner whose life of excess – wine, women, and song – covers over an ancient wound. He gets his desire met through manipulation: seducing and then abandoning; triangulating and playing off others. He attempts to completely repress his hysterical side, that is, his hysterical response to his own wounds, yet that "response" continually bursts out.[34]

The first figure, seen as John Reed in the novel, comes from the base of one's being when one is solitary. It's not that one is alone and knows an identity as alone. "Oneness" here actually is being fused with the unconscious of the caregiver when one is not humanly connected with her (I will use "her" as the primary caregiver here, since that most often is the case particularly after birth and in feeding). When one is abandoned, rejected, or discarded by the caregiver, one binds with her unconscious. That is an attempt for union as it forestalls such since what is available is experienced as more cruelty in the rejection. Yet there one becomes complacent, even turning the destruction on oneself, since the semblance is of union.

This phenomenon stems from the passage of wounds down generations. When the mother/caregiver, from her own childhood wounds, consistently cannot hold the child, be attuned and attentive to the child and his/her needs, ironically, the child is most connected to that caregiver's unconscious. The child is sitting in the nonbeing aspects of

---

[34] Arden, *The Articulate Silence of God*, 9.

the caregiver's unconscious – threatening impingements, harrowing phantoms, and cracked vessels.

Here is "Oneness" where one has problems in knowing that one exists in time/history and space/body. Here is when the infant or young child is attacked (that is, harmed or cut off or absorbed) so extremely that he or she is afraid for his or her life and experiences Death. Here is a fear of annihilation. Here is a devastating shattering, no solace or security, basic security needs are threatened, the very ground of being is threatened.

This is a problem in knowing one is an individual. It involves the caregiver attempting to swallow the whole of the child, in either absorption and/or annihilation: two people yet the experience is of oneness, only one there who matters, the other, the child, is nonentity. This problem later become compulsive behaviors involving destruction externally or internally as alcohol or drug addictions, gambling, eating disorders, and/or (depending on one's natural propensities and upbringing) workaholism. All involve experiencing oneself as nothing, no being, and grasping outside and/or incorporating something to attempt to instantiate one in life.

The only way then to becoming a human being, to being human, is to engage the world compulsively, even violently: the outburst of this caregiver's son, John Reed. He appears when the caregiver's unconscious negative forces, to which the child, in "Oneness", is available and may even prefer, cannot be delineated or spoken in any way and therefore seize the child bodily. These John Reed forces come from the bowels of the body: its lower extremities, its intestinal/ urinary system. Such seizures take the form of repetition compulsions (when the child is completely passive to them) and addictions (when the child attempts to lunge back but then goes under them).

"Huge cravings – oral, anal, genital – and releases are the John Reed seizures. No one speaks during them. The John Reed possession precludes (predates) signification and dialogue; It is an unmediated, onesided attempt to carry the unconscious to the world."[35] The child incorporates the John Reed forces, gives them bodily shape without knowing about them or their message, which is to be disembodied but act like a body. To act out these forces is not to be engaged with the world (what the acting out was intending) but to be pulled further into symbiosis antipathetically, further into the caregiver's unconscious.

Here, instead of being attuned with the caregiver's unconscious, it is to be fused with the caregiver's unconscious (dead) body, that unconscious that wants one not to have a separate, living substance or life: it is the deeper region

---

[35] I have been and will be using Afterword II in my *Lyrical-Analysis: The Unconscious through Jane Eyre*, to describe the three figures. See pages 333-349. This quote is on p. 334. Also informing this section is my work in *The Articulate Silence of God*.

of death and skeleton. This becomes the other side of the John Reed possession, the dead Mr. Reed force, the loss and symbolic or literal death of John Reed's father. Here, entrapped in the caregiver's unconscious, one experiences body as being a phantom, a dead body, cold and terrifying.

Others try to get the possessed child out of these realms by moralizing, which sends the child further into them. The child has to be met and accompanied in these realms and guided to speak them, find their word and message. Spirit is necessary to burn through the addictive nature of these releases, these seizures. But that entails true Spirit not the temptation of spirit discussed next.

Particularly daughters often have sought refuge from bondage in the unconscious body of the caregiver by an appeal to a Father Spirit to avenge the others, to rescue his daughter, split her out of the caregiver's unconscious: here is the Mr. Reed possession, John Reed's dead father, Mr. Reed.

Temptations of this Mr. Reed possession are fascination, anorexia, and appeal to Father Spirit for revenge. Fascination for the phantom is to feel special, chosen, preternatural and therefore desirous to stay intombed within the caregiver's unconscious. Anorexia is turning the tyrannical and death dealing force upon oneself to become literally the skeletal manifestation of the caregiver's deadness and desire for the child's union in death. Depression is underlying both temptations of fascination and anorexia, a deep, cold depression.

This attempt to appeal to idealized father also is an attempt to be a connection between the depressed mother and absent father. "The failure of that appeal is the poignant psychological crisis of the daughter's life: the descent of the ancestor (Father Spirit) which in the modern world is experienced and studied as hysteria."[36] Even in the heat of hysteria, it is very cold when Mr. Reed possesses: cold hell, the cold hardness of the edge of psychosis.

Therefore, behind this Reed figure, son and father, is the profound loss of a father. Loss through death, cold abandonment, and/or searing rejection. John Reed hungered and raged for a father. His mother hungered and raged for an attuned husband, a better Mr. Reed. The father has to be mourned with another who understands and who can help to word the loss. No father, no family.

The father in this culture is being depotentiated as he is asked to change what it is to father: from tyranny and domination to compassion and justice. As he is in this transition, this Reed figure emerges as the ones whom

---

[36] *Lyrical-Analysis: The Unconscious through Jane Eyre*, 335. Today it often is called borderline personality disorder. At this level, the being overcome by the Spirit Father is on the symbolic level, having to do with marrying Death in fusion with the mother/caregiver. See below for when it is emotional incest and physical molestation.

mother enfold children into herself when children often stay in bondage in the unconscious as a misguided act of love.

The healing for the Reed possession necessitates a speaking the fury of being made to fill the emptiness others experience (the loss of father). That is, not act out and become the fury (which regresses one to the Mr. Reed ice cold skeleton terror) but learn, with the empathic help of guidance, to speak it to an another, and see one's role in the cycle. Such adds to my understanding of Christ and the Incarnation.

A human cannot lift one out of unconscious entrapment in another. Christ is the Incarnation, and He can meet us bodily, go to the depths of these possessions, and accompany us out. If the human guide is knowledgeable about such, and in relation with the child, then Christ can work through that. The other side of the Reed possessions, their antidote, is an empathic figure who can hear and understand the effects of the possession, and, through grounding the child on earth, help him/her back to the human. Therefore, active listening and compassion, repentance, and longing, what I see as "the daughter" is necessary in this work with Christ.

Such empathic drawing out the death-call allows the dark figure of Reed to be suffered. It can be excruciating to depart from engagement in the lower will-to-power compulsions to attend to the midriff area of scream and pain: the suffering of one who only has lived in and through death, to feel and word that to the other who knows it. This is the "burning" of the Reed complex in the oven of the mid-region. Only such suffering, such "burning" can lead to an ongoing participation with virtue.

The vertical descent of Father Reed (his rule, his word, his omniscience) symbolizes the necessity of Word to contact the womb, to give form to, delineate, speak what is unconscious in the female womb, here, for men and women, is to speak the agony of being kept in death.

It is not just that Christ is meeting the child and helping the child to life on earth as human to breathe and live, but also to take the message of the unconscious possessions back to earth, to lend them to the wisdom of the world. Here also is my understanding of the Incarnation.

A certain strength is needed for the child to break the nursery bind, the unconscious desire to stay fused with the caregiver. It also is not to get tempted, as one resides more in humanity, to feed one's tremendous hunger by feeding on oneself which becomes an overextended giving out to others – over-giving, trying to fix or rescue others.

The second major figure, pertaining to repetitious family patterns and pathologies, is Brocklehurst who appears where the child's output, or creativity, is shunned and rejected outright. The caregivers attack what the child produces, what the child creates spontaneously. What is destroyed or attempted to be destroyed is what could otherwise produce the fruit of the Spirit, so the Spirit is attempted to be quelched here. The mode is of dominance. The attack is through searing criticism or being cut off entirely where the child feels its products are worthless, disgusting, and that he/she is rejected as outcast for them.

Here it is not a question of life or death, as with the Reed figures, but it is that *who* one is fundamentally is rejected, dismissed, criticized. It is a question of undermining and confusing the child's *identity*. Consequently, the child seeks an identity in a similar other to fill the emptiness and complete the self. Here is "Twoness" where the child seeks another, a twin, to stabilize and reflect itself, to bolster its identity, ego stability, and cohesiveness. Therefore, problems in identity occur here: seeking another to be one's identity and escape the loneliness of not having one's own.

Here one senses that the connection with the "twin" is crucial for life, and it is a beginning experience of eros. Such an education in eros is a crucial step in knowing Love. However, over time there is a continual battle for dominance with the twin in order to re-instate the self. So "Twoness" becomes the attempt to gain dominance leading to arrogance, obsessive contemptuousness, and competition. Addictions in the Brocklehurst possession include dominance over anything perceived as female, cognitive superciliousness, critique, and competition.

Possession by this figure also leads to obsessions in not being right or good enough, and a paranoia of being persecuted for whom one is. Whereas the Reed figure related to an attack on life itself, this is a rupture in one's relation to oneself. Acting out the pathologies associated with these figures are dysfunctional ways of trying to deal with the deprivations and those ways forestall going through the wounds and undertaking the suffering in that. Only though suffering instead of identification with these figures, can the ancestral patterns be "burned off" and a way to Spirit and Spirit's guidance through life result.

As suffering through Reed, with empathic guidance, was necessary to carry the child out of antipathetic symbiosis with the mother/caregiver, into a more lived human world, Brocklehurst is necessary to split the child out of a collective body which could be used as a resource for an identity without having or knowing a self.

To be criticized is to at least have an identity apart from the group. It is a crucial step in disengaging from symbiosis with another or a group, a collective body. Yet the Brockle-hurst splitting is driven by sadism including a misogyny of the female collective body. The danger is that in reactively resisting Brocklehurst, one has the impulse to go back and remain fused with the antipathetic body of Reed and unmediated discharge.

If one takes the Brocklehurst lesson instead of being possessed by it, one learns to rise in body. If one does not get caught by Brocklehurst in the neck-chest region of attack, condemnation, and competition, and instead suffers one's own defect, then moving through Brocklehurst can result in an acceptance of law, an understanding of justice and the beauty of the body as temple with head as Spirit. Here is the movement from Reed lower regions to know the upper body, to "sublimate" the driven forces of appetite, to see their symbol, and the Spirit that forms them to a healing. Here is the development of conscience.

The other side of Brocklehurst, his antidote, is a female sublimation to angel, to learn of Christ-Spirit, humility, detachment as identity. A female presence who knows the temple wisdom is necessary here to relate to the scolded, humiliated, wounded child and to guide to the embrace of Spirit. The lesson is differentiation within the collective body: how to be individual yet also relate to collective body. The teaching is to find the unspoken word of the Brocklehurst forces, to find where one is soiled, illuminated, defected angel. To go to one's defect and sit with the humiliation there, to lower to that, while accompanied by one of female wisdom, is to "burn" Brocklehurst in the oven of the mid-region. Only then can one participate fully in the virtue associated with Brocklehurst.

To submit to the ministrations of Christ-Spirit is to know oneself, and one's unique gift. It also is to find, through a female wisdom, one's individual conscience in heart. It is to learn how to prudently give to others. The experience here is of agape, which penetrates the first eros and prepares one for the next, deeper experience of eros.

How to manifest the gift one finds in this teaching is to begin condensing back down in body. Moving the gift back to body requires experiencing the humiliation instead of retaliation which is extremely difficult and counter-cultural. Condensing back down in this way brings up again the temptation of the Brocklehurst prohibition of female body as vile which has to be consciously dealt with for men and women to bring out the gift.

Another way to be possessed by Brocklehurst is to go so far up that one loses all body and dies. This could be detaching from oneself, one's body, in an essential Father idealization or to live as another body or to literally die. One has to take the Temple lessons back down and out into the world.

The move down, incarnating the gift, requires the counter-self, the other gender, now not Reed or Brockle-hurst. This involves the education of where our passion is still childlike, and how our will has to be exercised through a common-sense guidance, a practical attitude. We take the ancestral burdens down through realizing what they are and what they have been while holding on to a practical, grounded, human even mediocre perspective. It takes an education of will to do so.

Here is the third figure, Rochester, the education is of the will and passion.

The forces erupting after Lowood in the descent through body in wider world are spirits that are animal. Thornfield, as the embodiment of what in Lowood was the vision and narrative of otherworlds, is our encounter of the terrestrial, textured spirit, willful, driven, wanting its own way, the residue of Gateshead impulse now appearing through will.[37]

To bring the lessons of Spirit down the through body means an encounter with a driven will. To negotiate and own that will in a way that cooperates with the grace of Spirit, is to find the midpoint of Spirit and animal.

To locate, encase, humanly relate to that driven will is the way that Spirit, contacted in the temple education, is embodied in the world. It is the moment that the female (in all) who knows Spirit collides or encounters the male (in all) riding animal that no longer can go in its own direction. Here is an erotic moment. If one does not have the prior education and lived incorporation of agape, the force of this eros can be overwhelming and one can sunder under idol.

Rochester is a composite of Reed (his force and discharge capabilities) and Brocklehurst (his individual distance and scrutiny) as well as being other by inhabiting the body located at romance and heart. With the Temple lessons, we can move back down toward the Reed regions and dialogue with the male there. It is not to be gifted by him there, though that is the temptation: to leave one's own body and find another's gift which thereby circumventing one's own. To

---

[37] *Lyrical-Analysis: The Unconscious through Jane Eyre*, 347.

find one's own gift, through the dialogue with Rochester, his force and power, is not to use it as a commodity or be such a commodity for others.

If one meets Rochester without such Temple/agape lessons, and is possessed by him, then there has been an attack on the child's desire. The caregiver attacks/criticizes/ cuts off whom or what the child desires, longs for, who is someone other, desire for the other. The caregiver tries to take over the child's desire by becoming it. Physical and emotional incest fit in here, and the child's body and psyche then have to hold adult desire which overwhelms and can shatter the child.

On the adult level, having one's heterosexual desire controlled and manipulated by a parent or mentor for that person's gain, is within the Rochester possession, which is a fundamental betrayal of desire.

Here is "Threeness" and the mode is manipulation: where hunger, the oral, looks like genital so "Don Juan-ism" or promiscuity result. The addictions here would be of triangulation, getting into and requiring triangles to relate and feel. This includes emotional and/or sexual adultery, interpersonal possessiveness with extreme jealousy and manipulation, and seduction/abandonment scenarios.

The healing of the Rochester figure entails facing the terror of having another join oneself without the will-to-power defense of triangulation. It would be to stay with, feel and word the hurt of being in relationship, the abandonments and betrayals, the reduction of worth as well as the emptiness and loneliness felt when the loved one is with others. To do so with another who understands yet is not a substitute for spousal relationship, is crucial here. Through feeling through and communicating that suffering, Rochester can be "burned" in the oven of the mid-region. Then one can participate in the virtue associated with Rochester.

The result of not having a sense of who one is, being exiled from oneself, from being cut at through abuse or neglect, feels like being in a God-forsaken hole. The hole in the soul was noted many centuries ago.[38] Reed, Brocklehurst, and Rochester are misguided attempts to try to escape the

---

[38] What is interesting is that, in 523 A.D., from horrible circumstances in prison, Boethius, an Italian statesman and academic scholar, wrote *The Consolation of Philosophy,* which was considered, for the next 400 years or so, in the Middle Ages in Europe, as the most important philosophy book. Chaucer, Dante, St. Thomas More, Elizabeth I, all were extremely impressed with it. He is visited, while suffering mightily in prison, by Lady Philosophy, a female figure from metaxy. (Of course, given the cultural and historical period, there is the split female and Lady Fortune is discussed as negative). Lady Philosophy tells Boethius that the trauma of being attacked by the state caused a breach, a hole, in his soul into which anxiety entered resulting in his losing who he is, having exiled himself from himself, and thereby relying on false beliefs.

hole by will-to-power defenses, in order to try to hold oneself together, to not feel the dissolution, the falling apart, the havoc of being exiled from life, oneself, and the beloved. They are short "fixes" to try to stem the numinous dread of that hole and being within it. But possession by them only fragments the personality resulting in a further fall into hole.

Marie-Louise von Franz on psychic holes:

> Actually, when Jung discovered the complexes of the unconscious, he did discover them as dark spots, namely, as holes in our field of consciousness. By making the association experiment he found out that the field of consciousness was tightly put together, that we can associate clearly and correctly except when a complex is touched, and then there is a hole. If a complex is touched in the association experiment, there are no associations. That, therefore, is the normal view of the unconscious, namely that everything is clear except for those disagreeable spots of the complexes, behind which are the archetypes.[39]

I do not think that the complex makes the hole as much as the bonding with the caregiver's wounds makes the hole and that constellates complexes which are in the hole.

---

[39]Marie-Louise von Franz, *The Problem of the Puer Aeternus* (Toronto, Canada, Inner City Books, 2000), 161-162.

As I discuss in *Orbits of Symphony*, it is necessary to see each possession (and the resulting addictions, obsessions, and compulsions) as a call to sit in the hole feeling the depotentiation and humiliation and sense of exile. It helps to have such done in relationship with a benevolent other who understands the place and how one is in it. It is not to attempt to fill or propitiate the hole but to go through the rent curtain of the Holy of Holies to Christ-Spirit.

Suffering such holes is to be burning the debris, acting out, the sins, and destructions of one's own and one's ancestral past. This burning has to be contained through human relation, as stated, but also needs the grace of the Spirit, for it not to become bonfire. Here would be the redeemed Rochester integrated in psyche. Here is the other side of Reed, Brocklehurst, and Rochester emerging as virtues.

Again, acting out the pathologies associated with these figures are dysfunctional ways of trying to deal with the deprivations and those ways forestall going through the wounds and undertaking the suffering in that. Only though suffering instead of identification with these figures, can the ancestral patterns be "burned off" and a way to Spirit and Spirit's guidance through life result.

The danger is that if one then is not participating in the Forms to which each figure relates and points, the hole can attract other "false gods", other lower energies and defensive will-to-power reactions (Luke 11:14-16).

Jung wrote in his Letters:

Shouldn't we rather let God himself speak in spite of our only too comprehensible fear of the primordial experience? I consider it my task and duty to educate my patients and pupils to the point where they can accept the direct demand that is made upon them from within. This path is so difficult that I cannot see how the indispensable sufferings along the way could be supplanted by any kind of technical procedure. Through my study of the early Christian writings have gained a deep and indelible impression of how dreadfully serious an experience of God is. It will be no different today.[40]

These three possessions each are attempts to control and repress certain emotions. So, as stated, as one is working through the possession, in dialogue, the emotions flood up – the panic, anger, grief – differently for each one. These emotions have to be processed and understood so that the

---

[40] C.G. Jung, *Letters,* Vol. I 1906-1950, in *Bollingen Series XCV:I,* ed. Gerhard Adler and Aniela Jaffé (Princeton, NJ: Princeton University Press, 1971), 41. Also, see p, 345, to Herr Irminger, "…I start from a positive Christianity which is as much Catholic as Protestant, and I endeavour in a scientifically responsible manner to point out those empirically graspable facts which make the justification of Christian and, in particular, Catholic dogma at least plausible, and besides that are best suited to give the scientific mind an access to understanding…"

destructions from abusing figures within them can be mortified, redeemed, and then commemorated. Thus, emotion is a way to virtue, it is not entirely an issue of the mind or intellect or will.

To review: Possessed by the Reed figure, one impulsively acts out, greedily grasping for instantaneous pleasure to escape the death bind with caregiver in the terror and profound grief at the loss of a father; or, at the other end of it, possessed by Mr. Reed, one lives in cold terror in a death hold by the fallen Father.

Possession by the Brocklehurst figure, where one's creativity, giftedness, is shunned, comes with an attempt to separate from the mother, with whom one is bound in antipathetic symbiosis. Here one condemns and criticizes, trying both to escape the pain of and anxiety in her loss as well as the temptation to return to fusion with her.

Possessed by the Rochester figure, one acts out driven lust and triangulation to try to escape from the loss, humiliation, and depotentiation when one's desire has been manipulated, betrayed, and abandoned.

When one is identified with Reed, one reacts primarily from unmediated destructive appetite. When identified with Brocklehurst, one reacts from cognition that is slicing and cruelly competitive. When identified with Rochester, one reacts from repetitious seduction-betrayal manipulations.

Only through a human attunement suffused with the grace of Spirit, does one move up from Reed to Brocklehurst and then incarnate to the redeemed Rochester. Such movement necessitates accepting and embracing the suffering in each, without going under, through an empathic other with Christ working throughout; in such acceptance is the moment of grace which one can choose to participate with or not. If choosing to, then one is "in tune" with the circuit of metaxy leading to the Forms of truth, beauty, and goodness.

Reed, Brocklehurst, and Rochester each correspond to virtues. They are epochs of history, working out virtues. Reed – fortitude; Brocklehurst – justice; Rochester – temperance; and the humiliated, wounded, redeemed Rochester – prudence. Each come with the message how one is not aligned with virtue and therefore not participating in the Body of Christ. So here is blockage or dissonance in the circuit of metaxy, affecting the soul, holes in the soul.

Each is where will is not contained or limited by anything objective, by Logos, with its structure/music. Each is where one falls short, living in body not Body, preferring human self-sufficiency, will-to-power, cacophony. As such, each figure is numinous, forceful, commanding and possibly generating fear and even awe.

To not fall in or between them, into the hole of the soul, one needs a strong "identity". By identity, I do not mean only knowing who one is, but aligned with God, also to have self-awareness of one's vocation, one's purpose, and how one is situated within that. Also, it requires knowing oneself within a community within certain conventions[41]

In each hole, one must ask: To whom am I now bound? To what addiction, compulsion (mental or physical), person or job/duty/ambition? One is always bound in an attempt to counteract/fill the hole when one is not accepting the cross of it. This means to sit with, get the image of and feeling of being deserted by God. It is not as simple as putting God/Christ into the hole or trying to experience that. It is more to stay with the vastness of the hole and begin to feel the presence of God as an atmosphere in it.

As Marie von Franz continues in her discussion of Jung on complexes as holes in the soul, to see both sides of the archetype is crucial here in order not to not fall into the hole, possessed by the archetypes (literally die or kill in Reed; condemn or be condemned in Brocklehurst; seduce-abandon or be bereft/destitute in Rochester).

In discussing the importance of exploring the other side of the archetype, the dark spots, she says: "This is the typical compensation in a case where the ego is too weak to stand the opposites and see both sides of the thing, namely, that the archetypes are the source of illumination on one side but

---

[41] Note Jung's statement on the necessity of convention as related to spirit in footnote #22 above.

that one must also keep one's feet firmly on this world at the same time." [42]

Seeing both sides: when a figure appears, say the father in a father complex, as one is tempted to go under, what is interesting is that life itself will present both sides of the father – in people in one's current events. The 'good' father and the 'bad' father will appear in one's personal life. It is tempting to cut off one's father entirely due to the bad father's presence. Instead, it is crucial to hold them both which means sitting with, acknowledging, and feeling deeply the disturbing affects and attitudes emerging from the 'bad' father, seeing their message of similarity with one's own behavior and attitudes, and staying in relation to the 'good' father.

So in terms of renewing oneself: the loss with the Reed figure and landscape is that one is in danger of losing one's existence, literally and figuratively. The loss with the

---

[42] Marie-Louise von Franz, *The Problem of the Puer Aeternus*, 162; she is referring to Jung's use of the concept enantiodromia, from Heraclitus, that the opposites meet, are always present and can compensate for one another. So one must hold the balance between the life of the individual and that of the collective unconscious. Therefore, Jung says: "The ego keeps its integrity only if it does not identify with one of the opposites, and if it understands how to hold the balance between them. This is possible only if it remains conscious of both at once." Jung, "On the Nature of the Psyche," p. 219.

Brocklehurst figure and landscape is that one is in danger of losing one's creativity and spiritual foundation. The loss with the Rochester figure and landscape is that one is in danger of losing the loved one, the soul mate, the other side of oneself through abandonment and betrayal.

Each of these losses are different "holes" in the psyche that need different kinds of attention and healing. All need a benevolent witness.[43] Yet each consists of its unique anxiety and terror. Each has its own compulsions and addictions to try to fill the unique hole, and its failures in doing just that.

Also, in each hole, there is a different requirement for one to follow the indications of nature.[44] For Reed, it clearly is to speak the fury of being almost annihilated. For Brocklehurst, it is to accept one's defect and move to the Spirit in the temple of the world, 'higher' appraisals in the development of conscience. For Rochester, it is to get close to humility and woundedness in love.

---

[43] See Alice Miller's work such as: Alice Miller, *The Drama of the Gifted Child* (NY, NY: Basic Books, 2007); Alice Miller, *The Untouched Key: Tracing Childhood Trauma in Creativity and Destructiveness* (NY, NY: Anchor Books, 1990); Alice Miller, *Thou Shalt Not Be Aware: Society's Betrayal of the Child* (NY, NY: Farrar, Straus, Giroux. 1984).

[44] See Jung, *The Visions Seminars, Book 1*, 54, and Marie Louise von Franz, *Shadow and Evil in Fairytale* (Irving, Texas: Spring Publications, 1980). *The Feminine in Fairytales* (Irving, Texas: Spring Publications, 1979).

The hole has to be arrived at, accepted, and this is, in my understanding, to accept the cross and will to receive the divine grace associated with it. Different crosses encompass the three figures and different graces. Grace to be alive, grace to be creative, grace to be loved in an adult relationship.

The conditions that are ripe for the possession by a complex include loneliness, being cut off, feeling discarded, not being seen or recognized. One feels frozen, anxiety in the blood freezing, simultaneously feeling entirely empty while something continually is sucking one out driving one to compulsion. Feeling frozen, unable to act, and the events of life unfold in correspondence with the complex. It's not that the complex causes such life events, but that one, possessed by the complex, experiences the world accordingly. The divine plan enters here.

I will go to questions that I discussed in *Orbits of Symphony* and carry them further.

The question is raised: is the soul "whole" and then, with trauma, split into "fragments" each with its own character, i.e., a complex? Or are these "fragments" always there and connected, either loosely or not, depending on family genetics and behaviors, and trauma pronounces the differences, unties them further? Does the "fragment" split from the soul per se?

I see it that when one is identified with, to the extent of being possessed by, the "fragment", and thereby in a complex, one is identified completely with an "unclean" member on the circuit of metaxy and then one is split from one's soul. Here is "soul-loss", a degree on the spectrum of "soul murder".[45] These "fragments" are members residing in metaxy carrying unresolved familial moral issues and falling under their influence can lead to dissociation from one's soul and destructive action. [46] The way dissociation accompanies unresolved familial *moral* issues has not been understood in the trauma studies.

Returning to being consonant on circuit of metaxy and thereby participating in Christ's Body, is to have access to many wills oriented to virtue and thus attaining a flexibility and compassion of a flesh heart. The inmost being is what hid as the will-to-power beings predominated. No one, not even who is possessed and "benefits" from power, wants to inherit the dissonance of these ancestral beings. The more one identifies with them, the smaller and more inaudible the inmost being. Cacophony to no sound at all. Dissociation from one's own body and an uncleanliness pervades; dis-

---

[45] Robert J. Stoller, *Splittings* (NY, NY: Dell, 1973); Leonard, Shengold, *Soul Murder: The Effects of Childhood Abuse and Deprivation* (NY, NY: Fawcett Columbine, 1989) and the work of Bessel van der Kolk such as *The Body Keeps the Score: Brain, Mind, and Body in the Healing of Trauma* (NY, NY: Viking, 2014).

[46] See my *Starving Women; Lyrical-Analysis; The Articulate Silence of God; Clara and Marcus* (Bloomington, Indiana: Xlibris, 2002).

sonance on the circuit of metaxy. The figures remain complexes and dark holes reside.

Self-awareness is to know how one is, who one is, when one is cleansing through burning the 'bad' of these beings. The empty remains are permeated with the atmosphere of God, which satisfies, which "fills" so one knows the inmost being which, paradoxically, allows one to feel related with self and, importantly, others as the virtues are experienced and delineated. Without such relatedness, one is sundered and possessed in hole.

"Pathologies" Reed-Brocklehurst-Rochester: all three are attempts to move out of fusion with Mother and yet all ricochet back to it. Reed ricochets back through addiction and bodily nonreflective impulse and compulsion; Brocklehurst through arrogance and condemnation of the other, particularly the female; Rochester through literalized and triangulated erotic desire and enforced idolatry.

The mother protects the child from birth (and in womb) from dangerous forces and threats, at first from the external world and then from the internal world of the child, and next, when the father takes over the role of protection from the external world, the mother still can attempt to guard the child from unknown forces in the psyche. This gives her a God-like presence alongside being denigrated humanly,[47] which has led to great difficulties for men and women to

---

[47] See my *Starving Women* and *The Articulate Silence of God*.

separate from her in psychologically and theologically healthy ways, resulting in the misogyny of ages accompanying a fusion with her often resulting in one's taking on the historical pathos, the repetitive burdens of the soul.[48]

The work is to distinguish the various "split-off personalities", essentially arising from the Original Trauma of the Fall,[49] when one is traumatized by the Mother or Father instead of being protected by the parent, or, in some ways worse, traumatized alternating with being protected. Such split figures are dissonant on circuit of metaxy and either can impede or open one's way to Christ's Body depending on how they are understood and negotiated.

When the members are split and dissonant here is what had been seen as "split-off personalities" or "the split-off part of the psyche". Here is where one, as a victim of and/or defending from trauma, has identified exclusively with a member, leading to "loss of the soul" and thereby dissonance on circuit of metaxy.[50]

By "split off", I mean that one no longer resonates with these figures yet disavows them entirely which leads to being

---

[48] See *The Articulate Silence of God*.

[49] See *The Articulate Silence of God*.

[50] See my *The Articulate Silence of God*; *Clara and Marcus*; *"The Train" and "Jude's Wife"* (Denver, Colorado: Outskirts, 2015); *Unfolding* (Denver, Colorado: Outskirts, 2015); *Purcell Wrengt* (Denver, Colorado: Outskirts, 2015).

fused with them, thus possessed by a complex.[51] The trauma leaves serious emotional wounds tearing away parts that no longer are acceptable or are perceived as the cause of the trauma; they need to be brought back in synchrony, in tune, with the rest for health and a participation in Body. These disavowed parts are the ones that participated in the trauma (either being a victim of it and/or defense to it), they are caught in the repetitive familial pattern (or receiving the effects of the unresolved traumas of the family) and they also reside on circuit of metaxy. It is not that members leave metaxy since it contains all the person's members. It is that one's identifies totally with the destructive side of a member or like members at the exclusion of others.

Therefore, trauma often results in "pathologies" leading to both the fleeing from Mother and simultaneously ricocheting back to fusion with Mother. In the disorganization, there is a disintegration opening one to disavow (not able to accept, realize) some members on the circuit of metaxy and, therefore, be over-identified with (possessed by) by them or others.

As discussed in *Orbits of Symphony*: To work through its holes and return to soul, participating in a consonant metaxy, is to have heeded and worked through the messages of Forms working through such figures as Reed/Brockle-

---

[51] See *Starving Women*; *The Articulate Silence of God*; *Orbits of Symphony*.

hurst/Rochester, these will-to-power beings, to have found a language to communicate with them and experience the affects, attitudes, and motivations associated with each so that they diminish and are mortified and commemorated while becoming oriented to virtue.

To return to the soul is to give space between the person and the figures possessing, hear from where they orbit and what they want, to explore their intention and from what they were attempting to escape. It is to know in an embodied manner from what they were an attempt to defend and repress. This understanding requires a sitting with affect instead of identifying with it and going to one's vulnerability, a sense of weakening, even disintegrating, and appeal to God in that. Here is the move up the body, ancestors revived and sorted and quieted, and down the body to the flesh (broken, humbled) heart (Psalm 51; Ezekiel 11:19-21) leading to a change in action and life.

As discussed above, this sitting with affect requires doing so in relationship: with another or others who recognize who one is and who carry the grace of the Spirit in listening to and holding the pathos being expressed. Being part of a community, grounded with like others who care for one, during this work also is pertinent to the healing.

Once sitting with affect, one can find the images that are the core of the complex, the image in the affect. They often, when one is possessed by a complex, are difficult or stressful images, but, within human relationship, they can be seen, dialogued with, and understood. They are the obstacles to Spirit, the dissonant circuit of metaxy, as they are the way to open to circuit and be at one, atoned, with Christ's Body.

Therefore, complexes are how God communicates through Forms exerting a force on our body and soul, and how God is available to us, and grace draws us to God leading to a living more in virtue and thereby changes in the world.

In *Jane Eyre*: It is not that the mortified Reed, Brocklehurst, and Rochester are lost (which could lead to their sudden emergence later), they are commemorated: Reed in Jane's fortitude while the Lowood school is under attack within and without; Brocklehurst in her ability to discriminate and discern, through justice, later at Thornfield; Rochester (unredeemed) in her moderating her compulsions in passion, through temperance, leading to her understanding of love and passion as she relates to St. John Rivers and returns to the redeemed Rochester, prudently in marital love with the other side of herself. This commemoration allows her and Rochester to resonate with the consonant circuit of metaxy to God.

Now to return to basic definitions: Brontë's experience of the men in her life were her members of metaxy (her brother, her schoolmaster, her mentor/lover). Her genius was in seeing and creatively representing them beyond that of her personal life as figures: each with their own sets of relationships, affects, attitudes, pathologies and need for healing. That is when John Reed, Mr. Reed, Brocklehurst, Rochester are figures and appear in her novel. Since the novel has been appreciated and understood for generations across continents, the constellations of these figures are archetypes, representing patterns of experience across time and space. This indicates that she was able to tap into the Forms from where these figures issued.

The way that the figures had been problematic in life for her, and thereby could be for others, makes them complexes. Both the advantageous/beneficial and problematic/destruct-tive aspects of each figure are in Bronte's soul, and she had to work with them to find their resonance with Forms. Here is where morality enters into the study of figures of metaxy: there are beneficial and destructive, good and bad, aspects of each figure. The destructive, unclean aspects have to be suffered, mortified, and commemorated. That cross cannot be avoided if one is to, through human benevolent relationship and healing through Grace, live a healthy, bountiful life through Spirit consonantly circulating in the material world.

Reed/Brocklehurst/Rochester are "numinous" in sense of the Old Testament God, yet they violate. Reed is a murderous tyrant; Brocklehurst is a black pillar speaking fire and brimstone; Rochester is a possessive idol. One becomes broken from identifying with them, and realizes the need for cleansing, atonement. Atonement would have Christ be a shelter from them as an understanding of them which is the

Christian message in *Jane Eyre* of Mr. Lloyd, Helen, Miss Temple, the Divine Mother (seen in the moon in the Dark Night) and the Rivers sisters. Here is how Logos is Love and, through such, Reed/Brocklehurst/Rochester, mortified, and now commemorated in virtues, can become a language that is communicated in relation, which allows the space to inquire the "numinous" forms, take their lesson and orient to Body, which is to experience the vulnerability of the soul having carried and helped to transform the disfiguring, unclean burdens passing through the family.

STORIES

1.

THE FIVE

I.

In the somnolence she was quite awake, and she balked. She had been carrying the knapsack on the top of her back for a long while and the children in here had not died. She had thought there were three from Africa, but that was just a guess. WHEN SHE WAS OVER THE HUMP OF THE RIVER, SHE WAS GLAD AND SAT DOWN, HAPPILY, NOT SQUANDERING A MOMENT OF REST, THE RELIEF PALPABLE, SHE FLAPPED THE SOLES OF HER FEET IN THE WATER. JUST IN CASE. JUST IN CASE THE SOLES WERE DEHYDRATED.

There had been so many dry days of no water. She had thought the plants would be scorched. But even from distance, she could see them alive on her windowsill and far away, they seemed to wave.

And the cat who had always awaited her and had sprung to that window ledge at the sound of her steps, had been deceased, but the imprint remained. She could almost feel her do it now, spring up, without dislodging any plant even one inch, so graceful, so precise, almost French. The imprint of that beautiful cat who was long gone. The wavy plants, or, as if waving were still here. They were vibrant enough, even after the long spell.

She noticed it as soon as she entered the door which did not squeak nor was it peeled. Metaphor can only take us so far, she whispered to her plants as she carefully let the backpack descend to the linoleum.

It had been too dark for her at first, these tiles that brown tinged maroon that, though it hid the dirt, resembled something far beyond is glory, laden and remorseful. So the backpack landed and whatever dirt it had accumulated in the travel met the linoleum, a greeting not stirring either. As she was whispering to the plants: you remain vibrant, she recalled the children. Carried all that way, and yet they looked calm, looked as if they belonged in this very kitchen that they never had seen, that was no way within their radar of recognition.

She was happy then, happy in her own way. The remorse was in it, this happiness, but was more additive than diluting. Before she turned to the children, she reframed the question to herself. It was no longer "WAS THE TRIP WORTH IT?" but "HOW HAD IT LEAD TO HER QUESTIONING IDENTITY?" The concept, the reality of identity.

She asked the children to emerge one by one and looked at them in turn, without a word. No longer would she expend so much out of the fear that warranted a doubling of speech to soothe. They emerged and she felt like the old lady in the shoe though she had tried to abandon metaphor: there were more than three. More like five. After the fifth, she looked in to check and was reprimanded by the smell.

Though she had taken them out regularly on the trip, and they had discharged accordingly, she never really had counted them. The smell, therefore, was not of excrement or urine but the sweat of not knowing even while trusting. They spontaneously arrange themselves in a semi-circle around her now. She feels complete, nothing was missing, nothing amiss.

She fingers the fork she had gotten off the counter before she beckoned the children. The prongs are thick, thick enough for an ample cut of steak. Some children are singing far away and are not those in this room now.

She feels so complete that it is difficult to examine them individually, but she does so, in time. The time and the logic of it all does not escape any of them. Put a penny in the pool surrounding the statue in the center of the city and it will turn black after being green. Yet her wish, the base of the most primal desire really, had come true. It was the sanctity of it all that amazed her, so beyond her, so ordained.

So she examines the five now hers. They are gifts, they were divine minded long before they manifested first in backpack and now in kitchen semi-circle. And what is this notion complete outside of metaphor? The imprint of the cat whispered it after all. She did not hold any grudges, nor was she pristine in all her judgments.

As she replaces the fork on the counter, she thinks of all the ribbons she had fingered, twined, twirled in fingers of hands anxious and not, in the past. It had always been the ribbons. It took nerve this movement to fork, and to post-fork. She looks again at the children. They were not to be deciphered.

She holds out her palms and they enter the space, she holds the bouquet as gracefully as they enter and the embrace lasts long enough for the plants to remind her gently that though still vibrant, they still need water.

She carries the children and shows them their respective rooms. Two to two rooms and one alone. The singular one had preferred it.

The plants get their thirsts met appreciatively. Then she knows it is time to vacuum. It was a shame almost, she thinks, to have to subsume the residue of her time away, for this dust measures it, and, if it could be penetrated, probed, would indicate all that she had felt within that measured time.

But it was sucked up and the noise became rhythmic as the children slept. The bottle had come and gone, that milk was of another time.

II.

It had been so nice, she realizes she is afraid, some say, of the other shoe to drop. She notices, as the children are eating, that there still is an accumulated dust and sprays of lint beneath the legs of the table, caught and just peeking out of all four legs. She always had been a consistent cleaner who examined beneath such legs before washing the floor. But that was then. She sighed. She would learn to live with such accumulated dust balling now as pressed deeply. She resumes the cup of coffee; she smiles as the children speak.

She realizes that she desires a cigarette and cannot recall when she had given them up or had begun to smoke. The children are laughing at something. She realizes that she had reached for cigarette to silence the laughter that the children now over fill.

Children laughing. Blown up beach balls sailing through the air competing with the sailing vehicles on water waves. Sailing and hitting none now in the head, on the forehead, and the child laughs fearlessly. Not afraid that the peeling will instigate the jealousy of a repressed adult mourning lack of freedom. Not afraid of such retribution; laughing outright. LIKE A FREE CHILD AND THE ECHOES DO NOT EVEN WHISPER OF NARCISSISM.

So she had gone to the "dark continent" and when she approached home there were five children in her backpack. She smiles as she puts a lollipop in her mouth, pineapple and not homely, not pretty either. Simply not a substitute for the all-summoning cigarette, but a sort of interlude, wanting nothing from her and consisting of more fruit than sugar at least as advertised.

Her mattress had sunk in her time away; she noticed when she went to bed that first evening back. Perhaps it was from all the foreplay from the couple who had not been there yet desired to be. In any event, it had sunk where she slept. She was going to take the children with her to buy another, but she realizes that she has to do the research first. There are numbers and reviews to peruse, accounts to tabulate and figures to even out even knowing that no amount of foam could give her the rest required for those particular dreams.

She bought the mattress two weeks later and each child took turns jumping on it, signaling its firmness and grading such for her. She knew that each felt what firmness there differently and some experienced it as soft, far too soft.

III.

She recalls how she had painted a painting of them before they were born. She seemed to remember them from somewhere and the painting came along quite easily. It may have been a premonition or more likely a wish but one that had little chance of culmination at the time. She blows a sigh of relief. The painting had manifested in the flesh. This was not a tabloid or television screen effect. These children had survived the African desert. They were not scorched to death and now they were eating sandwiches in the yard.

Another template, another canvas. Slowly the whiff of smoke and the extended yearning for its meeting a parched and hungry throat dissipated. Her throat had been as scorched as the desert from the repetitions of choked fear cut off from voice, from percussion, echoing hear through halls there are good memories even from those most afraid who have hurt from prejudice from alignment on sides that no longer made any difference since were not the issue.

Hear the timbre. And no need to yell it when the tree fells. Simple bark of a tail without a wag, without a climatic resolution. They did not call her mother after all, but they came up to her with the gleam of eyes saying I recognize you for being the one sent to keep us alive through the penetrating love of existence. Cannot call it unconditional but close.

She drank the tea with them. It had honey and turmeric with just enough black pepper. It soothed their throats, a kind of guarantee and protection as she prayed it forestall potentially transmitted choke. The seclusion of the knapsack had been good for them overall, she could see it in their skin and how the whites of their eyes were not marred.

The children were swinging their legs in unison beneath the table. They chuckled with one another. Then she thought of the rope so useful then in tying the old knapsack, now jump rope. She arranged it on the pavement and then stepped aside. One at each end and three in the middle. She first feared that the buckle of shoelace draping their shoes might catch with a fall, dent or scrape, but then she saw their agility! What a witness. IT WAS NOT LEGS FLYING LIKE

SOME UPSIDE-DOWN CAUGHT BUG, BUT MORE
SYNCHRONIZED AND AS IF WATER SURROUNDED
THEM ALL, SYNCHRONIZED DANCE NO LONGER
CASCADE BUT THAT STREAMING OF CERTAIN
MOUNTAINS LEFT AFTER SERVING THE NEED.

She realized that they needed this release after being
wrapped in, contained, for so long as if in exile. The long, dry
trip with so few resources yet what was there was just
enough. The internal rhythm of the rope jumping cracked
through the air and she realized here is the release. Children
at recess yet not hidden able to exclaim, shout even. Dancing
bare legs open to make the air tingle at touch whereas before,
in the humidity and dew of the mornings, it had wept. Not
mightily but with enough pull to allow a consistent
dampness. Now it was clear the air liking the bare legged
dance very much.

When the showers came as they will. Come into the
garden child, and they went in quietly as if on tiptoes. They
regarded the yellows though not dandelion yellow more
squash and still possible for contributing to the soup. She
was watching from an upstairs window. When it's time to
make the passage to the next place, she saw it: go through a
garden gingerly.

The woman she had hired to help, from a case of poverty
and unfortunate circumstance, became her maid. She was
brunette and Greek and cherished the land though it was not
hers of origin. She had arranged the garden and she cooked

the fabulous soups with which the yellow flowers resonated and contributed.

This is to say that the maid came into the room with a cup of tea for her. She hadn't expected ever to have a maid and it was both exhilarating and calming. Some early undernourished place was touched.

She hunched over one of the five who had the toothache and who was crying on the floor. She was glad that the floor had been so carefully rubbed by the maid for it shone and it received the soreness of this child. Garbled speech due to the sore tooth. She held the girl and put a palm on the cheek on the sore side. She felt the warmth of the pain and it did speak loudly enough to hear even with her bad ear.

So the cold pack upon the very cheek and then the visit to the dentist who drilled and supplied the hole even though that in the child's soul, in all of theirs, could not so easily be supplied. But the five children together were a sort of miracle of healing.

The child eased into the dentist's tools thinking of the knapsack and Africa and being so close to her siblings and how no toothache was available then but that perhaps this toothache came from that memory. Even the child made the connection.

And as she looks at the child making the connection, she smiles and feels what only can be called a relief. AND THE RELIEF BLOOMED GRATITUDE THAT THE AFRICAN TRIP COULD RESULT IN THESE FIVE. She walked back from the dentist with the child hand in hand. The child was coming out of the anesthesia yet still wanted to jump and sing. The relief was that palpable. The four other children were playing in the backyard when they arrived and chattered as they ran to greet them both. So the tea party was unexpected but completely obtainable since both she and the maid bent themselves readily to the spontaneous ask of the moment, its request and its fulfillment.

IV.

When the knock on the window came it felt spontaneous but was somewhat disengaged. She thought it a bird's peck at first and then took delight in the understanding that it was human; a delight edged with the fear that remembers. It was not a consulting room, her home. She knew to give that up long ago. But the knock was real, real though disengaged, not seemingly part of any body or anyone she could identify through her sense of what familiar and what not.

She called out to the children to insure they were safely occupied. They were on the floors of two bedrooms playing jacks, playing pick-up sticks and Legos and occupied with focus and contentment. So she inquired the tap.

Tap tap tap, yes, it continued in reality, at the peak of some expenditure meant just for her. A compliment of sorts. But she paused. Thinking of the classics: spirits at the window. Yet its flesh tone both in color and sound said otherwise, not goblin, not ghost. The parameters of her search extended wide and then settled on this hand tapping, it was not accompanied by anything ghoulish or unkempt. She kept her bag for emergencies close to her in any case.

In it was the usual: band aids, antiseptic, scissors, tape and gauze, toothbrush and paste, eyeliner, a small bottle of vitamin water and another of vitamins, and various oils: clove, eucalyptus, tea tree and lemon.

She came closer to the window, the bag fastened around her waist. She thought she could see the vapor from her breath upon the pane, but she was not yet that close. She sighed. What does it really mean to get close to what hand wants one's attention? WHAT TO GIVE AND WHAT NOT TO LEND OR GIVE: THE PERENNIAL QUESTION WHICH SHE PUSHED ASIDE FOR THIS ONCE AND BEFORE THE KNOCKING COULD EXTEND TO THE DOORS, BOTH FRONT AND BACK.

Now she was close enough so her breath almost made its mark. She paused again – tell me, she said aloud, who are you and what is your intent?

The knocking increased. She held her breath. She listened for it at the doors but it was not there. She almost diverted her attention completely from the window – she listened for the children, did they not want her this moment, did they not seek her out – was there nothing that could reasonably in good time and good faith draw her from this window?

Nothing, not even a chirp from a sparrow on a branch nearby. Nothing, just wide-open space giving this perpetual knock a chance to be heard by one, by her.

She tightened her belt. She resumed her focus and she looked directly at the knock. The hand behind it was average size and could be male or female. She looked closer for telltale hair on it but its movement precluded definition.

Male or female, it kept knocking, rhythmically and with a pause between sound almost graceful. She thought of doing the dishes to sound it out, to cover it over. She thought of going to the backrooms to be with the children. Yet this in front of her was an adult requirement. Where was the maid: did not the knock beckon her as well? Yet she had left what seemed like eons ago for her holiday. The knock precluded maid. It was for her and her alone. Kitchen window knock. "Perhaps you are hungry?" – it was she who said it before she knew consciously that she would.

She engaged the lock on the window; once she disengaged that, the knock engaged her. She knocked back. Where the knock made contact at the window, she met it with a similar force. At first, they were successive, the two knocks, by only seconds, but eventually they became united, no seconds between, so it resounded as one large knock on both sides.

The cat, with them all from the start, walked into the kitchen slowly with a sly curiosity. Its presence did not revert any of it to a disengagement. Both continued to hit the pane simultaneously and in synchrony.

WHEN THE KNOCK COMES. SOMETIMES, SHE THOUGHT, IT'S BEST NOT TO OPEN BUT TO MEET IT IN ITS FORCE AND VELOCITY, NOT AS CON-FRONTATION YET DIALOGUE BECOMING UNISON.

The time had come, however, for the cessation and she asked it to show itself. She withdrew her hand from the pane and pressed her face to it as much so that her nose was distended and not in true shape. The knock had the choice: continue in a way, that seemingly would hit her face, or stop.

She breathed slowly and rhythmically in a tempo that her hand had used preceding the paned face.

The knock made the decision and stopped. She thought it a good sign that it wouldn't hit her even though the pane prevented such in actuality; a good sign that it wouldn't hit the image of her, the pane of her.

The tempo ceased and she held her breath again as she looked out into what now was darkness.

Then all was silent. She held her breath. She heard the children throwing jacks, the pitter patter of them upon the oak floor. She wanted her attention to be more with them than upon the pane and the recent silence behind it. She had to reel her attention back into the room. The fish landed in the pool of that affect, both lived and not lived yet.

V.

When she came out of the spell, the children still were there, and this amazed her. SHE KNEW HER OTHER SIDE HAD BEEN AT THE PANE KNOCKING, SHE KNEW THE PRIZE AND SOMEWHERE IN THE SPELL SHE HAD SEIZED IT. AND THE FEAR SEIZED HER KNOWING THAT.

She felt choked so she automatically reached for her throat. The dress she had on was paisley and guarded her privacy without being redundant. She did not need to be watchful on the mentor any longer, for she was that. Whether they all were accumulated in some interior dusty spot lodged beneath some table leg deeply within her, it was not a question. She carried them as she had carried the children, but they come to birth in different ways, still of the material but with less material substance.

Calling down the Forms, an act of love, she looked up and took the hands of the children, they made a circle. She looked up and then she looked around for everything she sought above also was around, and now was also within.

This circle had a total of six, she knew them all by heart yet least of all herself though that was changing. The somnolence began to cover her again, so she slapped her cheek so fast the children barely noticed. But one did. One had the best glance of them all, it was the one who would

have been in the concentration camp if he had been alive
back then.

He regarded her slapped cheek with amusement at first
and then inquiry: why do they, the five, continually seem to
put her to sleep now that they are at this home? He felt like
breaking out of the circle. He looked up once since he
expected an axe to drop. They all plummeted at that
moment; all fall down. They made a circle in the ground
since their fall lead them out of the living room to the outside
and on a different kind of surface.

Realizing that one's body has been sold out of terror and
letting another be one's body while something else got
developed.

She was sitting in the middle of the circle now, looking
them over. She reached out her arms. She wanted to hold
them all but first she knew she had to forfeit the adopted
body or else they could be used and used up.

She went ahead and found her own body and then she
sobbed internally releasing mentors and then she sat so
silently and still that each child could grow to go its own way.
They dispersed even as the circle remained.

VI.

When he came to the source of it, she thought she had
forgotten all about it. Somehow he had gotten through the
pane. She regarded him with a tenderness that was false

though not bravado. She pretended to open the drawer at her solar plexus. He looked nauseous and for a moment she thought he would vomit into it. But then he took the collar off his neck. It fell to the ground with a large thud as if it were a heavy leather yoke. She closed the drawer. He fell relieved into the easy chair.

She took off her scarf, knitted and softened, and put it around his neck since she was not used to seeing it so naked, so exposed. The she pulled off his socks. The scent was not discouraging. She remembered that she had to clean the lint tray of the dryer as well as the detergent cups in the washer. It was her duty to the germs. She wondered about germs on the inside of his collar. She looked down on it and thought she saw spikes, small, tipped, triangular and all breathing a relief to be away from his skin.

Sometimes she would think of his skin as leathered but that was just an excuse not to engage further. She had suffered the fall long ago and there had been no simple solutions. Seeing leather skin was only a small manifestation of the immense caution that was prescribed by such fall.

This was after that fall and after the five children had grown old enough to find places in the world that, even if not completely comfortable, did surround each of them with a sense, always somewhat foreign before, of who they each uniquely were.

BEING MORE THAN COULD BE, THAT A KEY. AND SHE FINGERED IT IN FRONT OF HIM. IT WAS LONG

AS IN THE OLD DAYS AND VERY RUSTY. WOULD IT
OPEN THE LOCK WHICH KEPT HER CLOTHES WHILE
SHE SWAM?

She licked her lips thinking of the supper she would
make him. She regarded the pot on the stove and heard him
snoring from the easy chair. There were no doilies any
longer.

Later they slept closely to one another and she clung to
the tarnish that covered them knowing the silver was safe
beneath it, hidden as revealed. She felt him lining her back.
It was a live flesh wrapper.

She reached for his hand to make sure he was human. He
was beginning to sense the five children though he didn't
know that. Much later that night she thought she heard him
crying in his sleep, but it was their large dog whimpering
while dreaming, even with paws twitching, while fast asleep.

The Presidents are all dead, she whispered before she
gave into sleep, before she worked her mind to the standstill
all the wet dried for this day and the lint tray was clean.

The dreams of that night fell short of her. She went
forward to make them longer but when she awoke, they had
flown away. She went back to sleep as though it was a long
winter's nap.

VII.

Her name had had tempest invisibly in it when she was young, but then it became temper and then it became temperate. The cost was high. She put her finger on his upper arm as he lay beside her. The fraught days were over. She knew something miraculous in her understanding. Before there may have been a divine mind of posit but now through the five she knew God. The temples were right. She was still sitting on the steps of one. She looked down on them. She assumed they would be marble but they were cedar. The grated parmesan cheese of the night before was still present through the taste in her mouth as she lay waking with her finger placed now on his upper arm.

He would not stir awake for another two hours. She went into the other room where the five children may have been if they were just that, children, fresh and open. But it was a while ago that they all had grown and moved. The old place was and would always have a place in her mind, the skin had grown over it. She didn't sell it but she moved through it. The thought of that time sat in her middle like a weight that carried lost tears to their source behind eyes that had seen beneath. There was some pleasure from there as well but that wasn't as pronounced as pound.

She heard the coffee dripping as she went in the dark side room to sit and pray and call on a saint favored that the day. She was not appalled today. The scratch on the screen from the cat who was outdoors and used to ice would not wake her any longer, but it had been a sensation of pleasure when she would let him in.

Don't let out the heat; don't let in the flies. But the children had grown, and the screen door was more dutiful now. And the maroon tapestry that the King walked upon was destroyed. Those manipulations, positionings of power, empty sacrifices were no longer needed, it was ancient history and she began to understand the new religion, the one truly blood blossoming from the many others before.

On her hem was a touch of dirt and a grass stain that may be easily enough removed once she knows the prayer. The hem caught the corner of her eye. She lost any sense that her thinking was removed from the very hem. Thought in hem, healing in hem, carrying forth and letting manifest the healing of that hem.

The room slowly will let in the light of day as the sun rises east. She knew that, there was no doubt. She knew her husband would awake; she knew that and there was only the doubt from knowing mortality. She knew she and her country would be safe, but here was more doubt than knowledge and that's when she thought of what defined safe.

This was the extent of prayer and it came to its full expression when she felt the safety in her bones no matter what. Then she sank on the couch and slept two more hours. They awoke at the same time. The purple socks were still lying at the foot of the couch. They have a scent of heritage and longing in them, which resonated with but surpassed memory of time with others in purple.

Time for Dinner! She used to call the children. As if it was a holiday but it usually was a simple eve. Ordinary. To the point. Simple repast not feast but in memory it all became that, memory making the ordinary feast.

And then she awoke and was saying the rosary. It was a hypnagogic affair; it had a certain way of coming up from the last dream and it rocked her while she woke. Mary Mother, Great Mother, always here, not only the virgin aspect of the Moon, but all three. Virgin, Mother and Dark one the last which absorbed her bitterness and regret. Mary dark one working through scent and vision.

The time of not understanding trespass was over. The time she was in the car of the new friend, she knew by the smell and the sick feeling when driving that the friendship would not take.

The troubadour began singing outside her window only yesterday. She went immediately to tell her husband and ask: do you hear it? The question was dutiful as well as seeking safety, the safety never taken for granted. He came downstairs to listen but could not hear it. SHE ASKED IF IT WAS FINE FOR HER TO LISTEN TO THIS SONG AND FIND OUT ABOUT IT WAS EVEN IF HE COULD NOT BE A PART OF IT.

He nodded and the look hurt her in its soft intimacy.

So she opened her ear to it, realizing that now it was not just Mary dark working only through scent and vision but also working through good hearing. She opened her ear and heard the song. It was plaintive as expected but something more. It had small bells in it, like the patter of the cat who had been out in the ice and who scratched the screen to come in and whom she let in with pleasure.

VIII.

THE TROUBADOUR SONG CONTAINED THE VISION. THERE WAS A VISION, HALF DREAM, OF ALL THE CRAZY KING'S MEN ON THE SIDE OF THE CARRIAGE, GUARDING IT. The song told that it had been a long ride and they were falling asleep. This was not the same as falling asleep at the wheel nowadays. They were not steering. They were standing and feeling the wind and the various temperatures. They were feeling these on their cheeks and also in the pit of their hearts hollow from so much standing in servitude to those they thought they knew, with whom they thought they were now intimate.

But actually, still the hollowness of those chambers. Some say yearning, others blocked or numbed or screaming, but it was all hollow. So they were falling asleep in the hollowness. They were no longer triggers in case some enemy snuck in. They may have had different degrees of hollowness since some had chambers larger than others and some had blocks that were larger than others.

What they had not yet realized was that the blocks were the same as the hollowness. But when they fell off the carriage, that was when they were starting to know that. Rumpled King's men and so of course the wheels had to stop. They slid into the dirt and the stones beneath them did not cry, realizing the necessity of silence.

There was no need of hospitals after all but a new employment. Some went to work in medicine stores and became devoted to endeavoring to soften the hollowness and allowing others to function with it. Some went to work in the chocolate shops to give others temporary relief from it. Some went into therapy and some went to the stars to go into the hollowness with others and some were able to face the panic there.

But at times these King's men missed the King for it turned out that they all knew him in their own way. They knew what he had for breakfast and how he had dressed for the day. They knew about his secret arguments with the Queen, not only because they heard that through the door but because they felt it in their very hollow chambers which resounded differently after such.

But today they all gather together as if for a card game. They are older now and the consequences of that growth do not escape them. They have barrelled through life it seems in retrospect but at the time it often felt excruciatingly slow.

They are sitting around a round table and the irony of that does not escape them. They are shuffling cards that are not playing cards yet are the sort that represent damages. Each one is an image of a different sort of damage and, on the back, its rectification. They take turns shuffling and dealing them out. When each gets one, they study it and think about how it relates to their time with the King and some very sores there. There are particular types of winning and losing in this game.

There are so few of us who actually fell off, one said, with a small degree of self-pity. But, another responded, it only looked like a fall, in our daze we were imitating it because the rim on which we stood was just too thin. Our boots were worn out and our ears were cold and cracked.

Yes, another agrees, we decided it and subtly agreed but it is hard to acknowledge that to ourselves. And a fourth: it is not just because we want to look like we are someone that we are saying this.

I know, said the first, but what now? What do we have to do with these rectifications? They sat in silence around the round table. One began weeping. It was #5. THE OTHER FOUR THEN AT THAT MOMENT REALIZED THAT THEY WERE WEEPING TOO, IN THE MIDST OF THE CARD GAME IN THEIR MOST HOLLOW CHAMBERS.

The rest was history. The King's men looked at the rectifications for the damage for a long time, but that was the extent of their vocation, their interest, and their pleasure. It was then a history trip for their daughters to take up the cards. One found one of the cards in a musty drawer in a remote closet. It was beneath birthday and get-well greeting cards. It was stuck between them and their envelopes and she found it when she was reaching for an envelope to send a birthday card to her close friend, the daughter of #5.

IX.

When the dream ended, she knew it had been the troubadour's song and she decided it was time to journey. The itinerary would be her own hollow chamber, the third ventricle. THE PUMP HAD SOUNDED TO OTHERS AS IF IT WAS WORKING SPLENDIDLY ENOUGH. BUT SHE HEARD IT DIFFERENTLY. A SPUTTER AT TIMES WHEN SHE SAW SOMEONE SHE WAS PASSING WITH WHOM SHE HAD TO SPEAK BUT DID NOT AT ALL WANT TO DO SO.

She had been lying in bed before sleep doing the new language lesson. She had fingered the page; it was sharp. She thought of all those who would not want her to go on, to be here. She took it in stride then she took the stride to the hollow chamber. It ignited some fear. She went into it knowing she had three human choices with which to deal with the fear: timidly and with apology to avoid repercussions, forcefully to put up a guard, or angrily to fight first.

She looked at her sleeping husband. She took hold of the steering wheel and she moved her tongue over her lips which surprisingly weren't as chapped as they thought they would be.

She was in the recess area watching the girls jump rope. She was by the swing and she was seven.

She is getting closer to the chamber. There are swishing sounds. There is a rise in temperature. There is a gentle touch of the back of another's hand on her right cheek. She started to take off the garments of criticism. She started to smell the baked cookies and then it became incense.

She got closer and then her feet went on the chamber at the top which was like a ceiling though a wall. Help me Mother. Help me Jesus. Then the front of her sole touched it. Too hot at first and the memory of some pathos of one she had admired which tore through them, and so she lifted her foot. Let it simmer. Someone is talking to her about tomato sauce on the stove, Sunday fare. Not so much the case in Britain but the romantic poets had tried to bridge that gap long ago.

She tried to put her foot on the surface again. She recalled her dream of the song about the five King's Men. It was not as simple as that the King, the President, the Minister, the Pope had died. That would be too easy. She knew now that it was for all to walk then fall and shrink and squirm and suffer and that was the hardest of all.

But intuition and wisdom were emerging from the lowering of power rational and mechanistic, and it was time for the King to know how very sick he is. The reparation, the rectifications that his men had their hands on would be taken up by their five daughters. She was one of them.

She collected the sons and daughters of the other four King's Men, and they sat in a living room with a hearth in which sat a wood stove. EVEN THE SONS AGREED AS IT WAS ALL LAID OUT CLEARLY. The time had been when the boys and men would watch football together, that was after the time they had hunted together. There was a relaxation in the bond as there was a unique release through it. The team either won or it did not win. The animal had been caught or not caught. The tears the men meant to shed were collected and rotated in a bronze soup dish. They each held it and knew that the contents were what they traversed and had tried to rise above but it was a sacred offering and they had to accept it.

Until they understood that necessity as well as the approval of it, they had to let the daughters take a turn. The clock of which the one who set and guarded it said so. At one time it was thought, BC in Greece for example, that there were many setting the clock and vying amongst themselves for the right time. But now the sons of the King's Men see that those were not the monitor and guard of the time, but they were the hours. Layers of generations understanding, through unwrapping veils, this clock.

So the time is for us, the daughters to take it up. The reparation, the rectification. The sons saw it and we all know that is unusual for usually there is a rebuttal, a push against, bringing the football game, the hunt onto the present table. Yet these sons were tired and had done the push against a lot, enough to know its futility and fruitless expenditure.

So they left the room. Truth be told, they were enough annoyed so that they did not bow or shake hands, but it was not a gruff or dishonest departure.

A ROOM OF WOMEN CAN BE A GOOD OR A BAD THING. They discussed the fact with which they all had had experience. They took the ribbon, blue velvet, that one was streaming through the fingers of both hands and they spread it between them, connecting in a way that bonded but not bind.

They took a drink of clear spring water with a tablespoon of red wine from the grapes prevent sour, no more sour grapes, no more fidgeting and confused nomenclature gossip with sly looks as one stealthily reviled the other at opposite ends of a hall walking in opposite directions.

How do we prevent that? The daughter of #5 was the one to ask it. The mother line in their responses to the father line rather dictate, squabble, competition fraught entanglement with sliced cuts between us.

They all asked: what would it be like for the men and women to work in unison without the women being mother or daughter of the men as it always has been? The privilege of being believed. It would be Cassandra not necessary to submit to Apollo yet connect after he worked through his despising of the dense darkness of the female fluids, finding, embracing. Christ with the women and behind them as they have their say.

#5 suggests they take a rest. There were separate beds for them, richly blanketed and with a fan in each so it would not get stuffy.

2

THE PIG

There is a pig here. A black little pig with scared wide-open eyes, wary of me. I want not much to do with it. The pig is looking at me sideways out of its right eye. Then I see a knife come from nowhere and slash the pig on its chest stomach area. It is on its side bleeding. I stitch him up. But then he is slashed again, a few times, back and forth.

Then, after much blood is released, a healing begins. The knife is gone, and the pig is on his side and healing. He is being fed by a bottle. I'm there, I put my arms around it. We cry. But I do sense that there is a deep healing beginning to happen.

When I awake, the pig is recovering in the crib to my right. We are in a sort of bedroom. I'm on the floor. I see the pig through the crib bars. It is breathing heavily but I'm not worried. I have untied the magenta and gold ribbon from around its neck. Then there was a pink one, and I undid that. I rub him and then put a little coat on him like our dog coats. I am satisfied.

I sit there. There is a large delicate mobile overhanging the crib. I look up at it and it wants nothing from us but just keeps on being there and I see that it would only slightly move if anyone moves in the room or if the door opens.

I think of the black baby carriage outside on the sidewalk. I'm in this room which is on a second floor. The windows have bars on them in intricate designs. As if someone out there would want to come in. The expansive view no longer is necessary. Once one had said that he could understand the Fundamentalism of the place because of the way storms could tear through the flat, wide expanse.

Now, decades later, I recognize such Fundamentalism as Brocklehurst defense to wound.[52] The mirage is over. The curtain has come down. The audience applauds and I am chilled to the bone thinking of the repercussions of their stimulation. When stimulation becoming provocation or worse – the drive, the pull, to look behind.

The pig is sleeping soundly. The band that had been playing in the streets has paused. Maybe they realize that the baby in the black carriage below was asleep.

A nurse is at the door who wants to take the pig's temperature. But this nurse thinks that the pig is a baby. She does not realize that the human baby is in the carriage below, but she knows the "baby" in the crib is recovering and had had mighty blows for which blowing a kiss to it would not suffice.

All the ribbons I have woven through my fingers, but I have to resist the temptation to get another one. The feeling always was silky. She asks to come in. I have to tell her the

---

[52] See essay at the beginning of this book.

truth. It is a pig, a little black pig who had had scared, wide-open eyes and was wary of me, before getting slashed. She looks surprised and a bit revolted both which she tries to suppress.

The fingers on her right-hand twitch by her side. She rubs the fingers on her left hand through her hair from her forehead to the band that collects the rest of her hair. This makes it look like her hair was teased as in the older days. She gives me a questioning look. Still want to come in? I ask.

She replies: I have to look upon and groom and minister to my patient. My raised eyebrow says: even a pig? But I don't say anything. I wipe a potential grin off my face. I see between my eyes a desert that has one flower in it. A deep rose color but it is a petunia. The Princes were helpful for a long time, but they have gone. I'm going to see this to the end and not close the curtain too early.

OK, Deep Rose, you are with me now and we can let in the nurse. But first let's make sure that she does not have an empty stomach. I get up and go to a little refrigerator in the room to my left. I know that it is strange to have a refrigerator in a bedroom but there it is. I take out some provolone cheese, a triangle of it, and get some crackers from a box of assorted ones on the top of the refrigerator.

I offer the cheese and crackers to her but when she nods negatively, I tell her how important nourishment is for her now: the pig was very wounded and gently is reorganizing. Please, I say to her, go in fortified.

She does something I didn't expect: she sits on the floor, cross-legged, to eat the cheese and crackers. The cheese is a little strong for her, sharp in scent and taste. I wonder if she has a daughter. I seem happier for the wondering and do not have to know for sure. There never is another human completely capable of taking care of us and I think it strange that I don't care about what sort of mother she was. That will work itself out.

I feel deeply restful now as she sits and eats. She hands me the empty plate. I ask her if she is thirsty. She is about to say no but then stops. Yes, she nods. I go to the small refrigerator and take out a bottle of lemonade, asking her if it is too cold. I pour it in a little paper cup from the group lined tall on the refrigerator's top and leaning against the bookshelf there. Leaning tower.

She drinks the lemonade cautiously due to its coldness and also to prevent slurping. The time will get too heavy, we both know, if she does not get to the crib. She fastens her belt again on a new notch, closer to the center. She wants a cigarette. The surreal thought comes to her about whether she has defecated that day. But as she approaches the crib, the black pig wakes and that becomes her focus. I sit, now in my own crossed leg position, very still, holding.

She lifts the pig very gently to look at the stomach gash. That earth had opened and there was no earth goddess there and this time the daughter will not fall for the narcissus. The daughter already is in the pit of this wound and knows it well, has a certain certitude and comfort there.

The room suddenly becomes very cold as if ice is all over it. Like ice from the outside in though it is not snowing out. I hear it on the roof first, it feels like a cracking of my skin and yet it is a sound. The nurse still is bending over the crib. I see a thick lace trim on her skirt. I have no desire to either approach it or be put off by it. But I do want her to know about the ice. She has not yet heard the crackle; she is very focused on her new patient.

She reads the temperature and then she fixes the bandage. She takes up a magazine lying on a side table beside the crib. She begins to read a story to the pig, a story in verse form. I stand up – I go to her and ask: Do you feel the cold? Do you hear the ice?

She looks at me as though I have landed from another planet. I notice for the first time how thick her eyebrows are. I claim their notice; not the eyes but the brows which show an emotion different from that coursing through the eyes.

Then she loosens her buckle. Next she goes towards me in a way suggesting that the pig was never there, that the pig did not belong in the room. I think about Nothingness. I think in conceptual terms to defend myself from her encounter. There is a certain vapidity around her, but I will not dismiss her as others have and will. I stand my ground. It turns out that she goes through me. She ends up on the other side of me, behind and actually leaning against me. I bend towards the pig. It is sleeping, entranced in a way. I ask her: Now do you hear the ice?

She still is leaning on me somewhat. She says: In the glass? No – not little ice but big ice, surrounding us on the roof. She asks: About to cave us in? (But there is no tremor in her voice.) No, it is to do with the pig. That hole in his soul from being struck and from knowing he would be struck.

She asks: Has the ice come to redeem that? No, more to protect it, I say. Protect the hole to see what can grow from it, be in it, and grow out.

We sit side by side in chairs now with our eyes on the crib. We are waiting to see what grows out of the hole within the struck wound of the black pig.

II.

The tempest that could come out of the hole is absorbed by the ice after all. It is a vast homecoming. It is as if two twins on either side of the globe found a way back to one another. There is a certain delight in it like being at a carnival. When the moment strikes, it strikes on pitch.

Tempest absorbed and the pig moves just a little. It had been so still that the nurse thought its breathing was succumbing. The ultimate loss when black pig succumbs, yet when the pig opens for the tempest deep in the hole to emerge, to burst like carnival fireworks, then the breathing resumes and the pig will live.

The pig will live, that is, unless the tempest turns back on itself and burns the pig out. Yet the ice is there, covering over in a sort of consolation no one would expect. Then the nurse watches as the tempest meets the ice and the pig moves more. Just little twitches of the little legs. The nurse knows the importance of silence in times like this. I look up also, I see the tempest meeting ice. Twin meeting. The sound of it! Cascading ice slivering.

Then the boom followed by the silence that is beyond hollow. It is a void with a magenta lace lining that reminds me of the nurse's hem, but darker, but richer. I get up to turn on the light. Who would have known that the pig could accompany, bring forth, such vastness?

Nomenclature. Honesty with the grand gesture. A woman comes through, all aspects of the moon plus the sun leading to a culmination. A soft steel gray that will not, must not, puncture. She beckons and the void is a home. Her casa my casa, your casa and theirs also. Does the nurse know this woman voiced forth? I ask it to her two brown eyes: Do you know her?

The nurse is too focused on the pig to answer. But she has more life now and even is vibrant. The nurse has earned all her degrees. She has taken the polite steps up the required ladders without even getting a splinter. Her nails were painted more than a few times in the process, and she would hold her breath even more than that. But now she breathes steadily into the pig's truncated breaths, his staccato pulse regulating what can.

How she would dress up this pig if she could and she would scent him with jasmine and soften his spout with honey. And when the pig would go to lick the honey off spout: here the rub. Here the third degree. It turns out this pig has no interest in honey but seems to be connecting with his little hooves. Once they had mud encased in them, how he wanted them clean! But it was not up to him, it was actually beyond him. Given the space in the crib, his hooves are more evident to him. And he is up to moving them now, he is up to twitching as these legs revive, find their blood, and their momentum.

The nurse senses that the pig has begun a process of movement and she is relieved, sensing the impact of this step, she pauses. She wants a cigarette again but that would be out of the question. She gets into a dialogue with her dopamine pushing at the borders and she comes out at top. So she is quietly sitting by the crib.

And then the ice melted as the night preceded. I would have expected a waterfall sound or worse, avalanche. There had been so much crackling, so much cold. My blood is going slower in circulation from that cold. I collect myself; I wrap my already oversized sweater around me. I sit hunkered through the night. The nurse, on the other hand, is unyielding. The nurse perseveres, mostly standing by the crib and occasionally sitting there throughout the night.

And the little pig begins twitching his nose as if he wants to express some sort of gratitude to her. The water is going down the outside wall. I could say flow or surge, but neither would be correct – it's a kind of steady release, steady yet definitely a release, the sort of expulsion after being solid and even stuck for too long.

So I'm sitting, hunkered, listening to it, probing the occurrences that had happened beneath it for a night and part of the day when the black piglet had appeared. Now I can call him piglet since that certainly is what he is, who he is. It never comes full blown, such a pig, but little by little and it's there. His snout had been running then, so certainly his immune system was not up to being knifed. It's amazing he didn't die. I want to ask him his role in the knifing, but I dare not call out what struck traumatic.

The nurse stirs asking me, even turning her face to me to ask: Do you hear the raining, it is really extreme. I'm surprised that she didn't register the ice, that its bitter temperature is not in her veins as in mine. I say: I believe it is the ice melting. The ice from last night when the pig was so sick.

Oh, well, she says, at least it's not a storm passing through with winds that could strike us further. Further? I ask. Well, she says, like this little one was hit, though that a knife, it came like a malicious storm attack.

I tell her that she has a lot of empathy for him. She tells me she appreciates my comment and says that she is in her element here and she truly cares for the little guy.

So we sit quietly listening to it, it's fierce enough this release siding the building, but it is not a storm attack.

III.

And before one could count to one hundred, before one could know it, so to speak, we were in the park. It was one that might be dangerous at night but this one was not dangerous at the moment since it was daytime and the sun did not betray us, it shone, it was not coy or misleading, it shone. Cassandra had her consumption after all and, after a true courting, no deals, no quid pro quo, the sun shone.

The little black pig was at the end of a leash and was squirming. All his muscles were functioning now. The scar across his chest radiated bright pink when the sun would sneak a peek.

He sneezed once, this pig. I remembered the dinner party when the spouse disappeared, and the cat defecated in the corner of the room in which we were eating. A strange affair. One of the guests now is dead. But the pig was alive and sneezed that way in the park. It had disengaged from the crib somewhat unwillingly but willy nilly it wanted to live after all.

So the nurse was no longer necessary yet she stayed on. She stayed through the nights, and when the pig disengaged from the crib, she put the medication away. She stored it in the medicine cabinet in the adjoining bathroom, hoping never to have to see it again.

Such a recovery comes with a ripple effect, and the pig almost fell twice as he began walking again. Once was down the small step separating the two rooms but the other was down a flight of stairs. He would have had quite a hit so fortunately his heart was not leaning towards dying. This ripple effect was from the deep wound sounding itself forth, getting its vibration right, registering it in the world.

Now the pig walks carefully, gingerly, around the picnic bench. The nurse sits in the middle of it, nonplussed. As the pig goes around the bench, the nurse lifts up her arm so the leash does not get caught. I wanted to ask her why she stayed. I wanted to see if she actually wanted to stay or if she felt obligated to do so, as if she was in the military, that kind of duty.

She held her chin very steadily as if she sat like the center pole of a merry-go-round. She felt the saliva around her tongue. She was glad that her throat was not dry, yet she was not sure how to swallow all that had transpired since she had entered the room of the pig. On another plane, she was hanging sheets on a clothesline and the pins were wooden and cloven. She had longed for the domestic entry but that was not to be her slot, so she lived there other-planed.

I am watching all of this and surmising. I am remembering the past afflictions in friendship. I do not know whether I dare but the pig rather requires it. There are to be no more ribbons or ribaldry. The little thing does not even have a collar, instead the harness hook with leash. The pig is like a cat and dog together, it misses giraffe, it will never have the long-necked vista or the great gallop. The pig is black and thinks of what never can be. I am watching them. I am trying not to observe or predict but just take it in, like a scent.

IV.

Back in the bedroom and the pig back in crib for a nap. I sit on the rug where I have been before. The nurse knows intuitively that she no longer is needed by the crib. She moves her chair from there to where I am crouched and welcoming the familiar boredom out of which I do often yearn reaching for others to fill, to spill. But I hold my own with her. I do not extend.

She asks me the logical question of whether I would want a chair. Nodding no, I see myself reaching an arm to her so she would join me floored, yet I do not. What is she saying now? Something about a floor, a mop? I leave to hear her. She says: I should get another sort of detergent for that floor; it still feels sticky. I ask her: Which? Which floor did you say? The kitchen. Are you house maid too? Who hired you? From where did you come?

I was wondering when you would get to it. Your aunt, long ago. It was a time when women would wear hats outside and get away with it, even though it was easing out of being normal, it still was possible. She had that soft wool brown beret with the swirled design pin on the side. Becoming.

How did you know her?

We shared a taxi by mistake. I was there on the curb at the time and she thought I was someone else, someone she knew, and she asked me if I wanted to share.

Then you got to know her? She replied: Just casually, but she remembered me back then when you told her about the pig.

So the pig is not just here now, it was there then. It was at that point that I realized that the pig could be outside of time as it was in time. I ask: And she hired you?

They always do, the aunts.

For kitchen cleaning too?

And feeding.

I do extend my right arm. She shakes my hand, she is not disturbed by our exchange and I am not flattered which is a change, feels good, feels right.

I stand up. I go to check on the pig. He is sleeping with a slight whistle through his nose. As I look on him, a sharp yet brief disdain of myself moves up my torso through stomach to chest so when I look at my hands, I recognize them, yet do not want to own them as mine. How to live with pig and accept myself, or know my relation to him without repulsion for either of us or the nurse?

I silence the voice that says the 'not possible', the voice that is the small boy in a hand-made cart in the middle of a neighborhood street. When such was possible. When children played outside freely without an adult worry of their being harmed. The boy knew pig, nonetheless. Freedom in the outdoors does not preclude pig.

But I realize I do want to dress him up.

The nurse is standing beside me now at the crib. I want to put my arm around her waist. She knows the desire but forestalls the intent. She sees the boy on the hand-made cart; she is the girl on the scooter, the European, small scooter. She rides by the boy. She is recollected and smooth. She does not care about the smells of old people or the rot of stuffed disposals. She feels free though she too has known the pig since infancy.

Together they think of what they could have done better in recent exchanges with others they thought they were helping. I decide to take a nap. The nurse resumes her seat by the crib and is reading a magazine. Hats are coming back for women, she says.

V.

And upon waking, I saw the bright calico cat slither kindly to my left and down. It was fleeting but persuasive. It was like playing the stock market this determination of whether asleep or awake, whether actual or imaginal. But I knew I was awake, had been sleeping yet now awake. And I knew it was imaginal, this cat, clearly aloof. I saw the begotten of all my days in that full swoop. The revenge of the middleman no longer could swipe at me or take my breath away. As I had stopped swiping at flies long ago though the buzz sometimes did take up too much of my mind.

The licorice taste of it, that taste I once had concealed since it was so sweet and prognostic. Hiding in the tiny room, reading about St. Joseph, and seeing far ahead while listening to the man who bent concave to help me and who saw far ahead. The dangerous bent of seeing ahead. Sometimes I would think it is better to stay in the tiny room, repetitively, but I'm over that now and realize the pig has come from going too far out but that that is not necessarily a bad thing.

I snapped in my seat belt and looked for the cat. I sensed the cat knew pig and they had exchanged a certain sweat once, on the farm, within the coveted garden, unassuming, alone together.

And then the cord snapped, and I was in my bedroom on the floor and she still was in the chair by the crib. All the mothers who would so like to take pride in their daughters but just cannot due to such an array of triangulation and dust. So the nurse had not been recognized by mothers, I knew that as soon as I saw that she was chosen to meet the pig. That would have been enough to tell me. But to nurse him too, well, there had to have been quite a large degree of misrecognition.

The time we all suffer for, I startled myself by saying it out loud. I shifted my foot on some imaginal petal. The engine roared and I laughed. The time we all suffer for. I had said it, she turned abruptly to the left, staring at me and, in catching herself doing so, took a step back in her heart and breathed deeply, diaphramically. Not that she did not want to run to that window and leap out. But there were at least two chairs she could choose to sit upon at this juncture. To her credit, she didn't come to me to split me off and release herself from the necessary suffering. The cat was beautiful.

VI.

So the nurse stayed in the chair by the crib and I asked her if she knew the cat. Which one? A perfectly understandable response. The bright calico one that sort of floated by a few minutes ago. No, I was daydreaming while looking at the pig, of how he would look as he got older, of how he would fare.

Is he our pet now? I was bound to ask it at some point and there it was.

I suppose so, though you and I hardly know one another.

We know one another more than we know most people since we've been through knowing the pig.

I suppose, like going through a war together.

If we had cast him aside, it would have come back to us as a boar. We would have been destabilized, poor, lonely, and very stuck.

I know what you're saying. She turned and, still in the chair, looked at me, saying: It is no longer a time when people can keep themselves drugged all day with smoke and altered substance, dopamine enhancements. So the atmosphere is such that there are a lot of pigs like him appearing.

But he is ours.

He is yours and in coming to help, he is mine too.

I wanted to close the top on something, like a plastic tin of pepper. I wanted to hear it snap.

She jerked in her chair, but it wasn't because of that – the pig had awoken and, for the first time, the nurse saw the cat.

It is beautiful! She said so with genuine animation.

Does it have a collar on? I myself thought it was a strange question, but it was the first thing to come to mind.

No, and so sleek, so gliding and without a glance in our direction, unafraid yet delicate. It surmises what it needs to know in senses that we do not recognize.

Or care to know, I added, dealing with the pig is enough.

She looked over at the pig at that moment.

I'm so tempted to dress him up, but I know that is an inexcusable escape from him, from who he is.

I want to hold you. I was totally turned towards her now.

She pretended not to be surprised but I saw a slight jerk in her left shoulder. She swept some hair out of her eyes. Most of it was in the same rubber band covered with the pale salmon cloth, but some had wandered. She caught it to give herself a moment to recollect, to think.

It would be another escape. He's come for us to know him more than one another. Or – we will know one another more as we know him.

I'm sorry. I was just sitting on this empty floor and felt the need for contact.

The pig is about that.

How do you know him? Besides my aunt calling you.

I've escaped such pigs before so many times and had to deal with boars and I'm tired of being swept under huge hooves of nonsensical forces.

All forces have some sense, I thought and then said.

Yes, the sense in that nonsensical was to tell me not to escape the pig again. So I am nurse, his nurse, not yours.

But in being his, you are being mine, right?

That's the question. He appeared to you first but that drew me in. It's not a question of rights or ownership.

VII.

And the cat? Appeared to you first, she said, and now it is mine too.

Yours? I have raised my voice. It is not even here, I should say she. She is not even here. I know it is a she, I felt it as such. She is not even here – she is no one's – she glides and has disappeared. Beyond Ephemeral. She does not even eek of fake.

Why all that emotion over something not there?

It was the essence of her.

Like a muse?

No, even you are more than that.

Now you speak as a man.

I speak honestly. I am a tree. I have rings.

Enough abstraction. The pig wakes.

We still have to ask his relation with the essence cat.

Yes, she said, I was wondering.

This isn't hot chocolate on a winter evening. White Christmas. It is the one in the inn's manger with animal smells and a dampness.

I know, I know.

She is lifting the pig now. Actually lifting him.

I am in charge. I am beside myself with game. I am gaming. I feel myself get very far away from myself. I am becoming fake.

No one will call me mother or grandmother this way, she is saying it.

I put my head down and my chin is on my upper chest. I am magnified by my loneliness and my pretense and become aware of it. That is the pig stirring.

And, she asks, what is the pig being in my arms?

A joyousness not feigned yet covered by habits of uncleanliness.

I care for it.

He cares for you.

She is walking to me now and she is handing me the pig. I am amazed at the distance between the pig and my torso. My arms are supposed to be the bridge, but they were not constructed for such. I have been carrying this pig my entire life, I do not want to hold it. Its eyes may get fearful and it might bite me. The passages are clogged. The virus sometimes wins. So I remain defiant and still.

The pig could fall in the small gap between us but it does not. I smell it, and it is not the strident smell of a pig that I expected, of which warned. It is the tea tree scent, becoming an almost turpentine scent. It is heavy, poignant, and entirely free. And the pig is almost free. The pig now knows its own appetite and will not have to consider on any level to consume me.

The cat is approaching the crib and we both see her. We are in the corner to the left of the door entering the room. The nurse had come over to me during the night. The pig is safe in crib without my purview now, she said. So we together went into the corner to be close in this vigil. It was not physical, but all of the heart since we both still missed our mothers, the ones for whom we always reached and could not attain.

Much later, I awoke and saw the cat approaching the crib, so I woke up the nurse and we watched together. So nimble the approach, what a daintiness but was there a snarl beneath? Would anyone know the reason behind any of this? The cat lifted itself with front paws on the bars. The pig's meeting of the cat came forth as love dessert just emanating between them. Don't think this was an affair, but the light clothes I had on began to sweat and there were no splits now. The cat licked the bar. The pig snorted and I was happy.

3

DAFFODIL AND BLADE OF GRASS

The sweet side of the one blade, so green almost mint, speaks, as you can surmise, softly. The daffodil screams it did not commit the crime. The blade actually empathizes yet cannot be heard.

B (Blade): I came to see you yesterday and you weren't home.

D (Daffodil): I was home, I didn't hear the knock.

B: You must have, I knocked loudly, I wanted to get in.

D: It's time to take the temperature of this relationship?

B: There is singing in the forest.

D: Bats and mosquitos.

B: More vividly, a song, a cherished song of the forest.

D: The relaxing, the forest is relaxing.

B: What if you never hear me knocking at the door?

D: What if the forest catches fire?

B: I love you; I want to stay by your side.

D: Hear the ancestors clapping? Hear the saints?

B: The song of the forest.

D: I will paint a dog for you, a chihuahua.

B: Not a bulldog?

D: I couldn't hear the knocking.

B: The delicate mesh, don't let the dog get caught.

D: The dog was caught a long time ago, the dog is thirsty, its tongue is dry.

B: The rejoicing that the mesh can be there, and the dog can drink the lucid water, that the dog can breathe.

D: The dog can breathe, and we don't have to own him.

B: Or her.

D: Yes, our hands are sweating together. The violets have faded finally, and the other daffodils have screamed their last, but now, hoarsely they whisper. Do you hear?

B: Yes, and the stallions are in another country.

D: And their hooves are molten tough; the dust and the deranged mind of desperate, drunk cowboys do not hurt them.

B: What do you want to claim? The streets are empty now.

D: I want to unite with you in God.

B: I cannot be your God or a conduit.

D: Our union is of God.

B: What can that mean?

D: Do you see the road? The streets are empty.

B: But there is a great calm due to that, do you hear it?

D: I no longer hear the song of the forest.

B: It is because of the Great Calm that has come over us. Even that small pool of water there has not a quiver.

D: Yet it can get too quiet.

B: There always is the rhythm even in the most quiet, hear it?

D: The heartbeat...

B: The doctors see through a screen.

D: The scream within, most do not hear the inner scream of the doctors who want to cry: I do not know!

B: The doctors are an adjunct and they had thought they were the main driver, so they too are mourning.

D: Can we help them?

B: We bring our union of God to them.

D: And what could that mean…some kind of hatred has to be addressed that all that power wants to cover.

B: And the stocks and bonds. Money trying to cover that hatred.

D: Can you know what heals the hatred? Can any of us know?

B: The blackness in the heart we all share.

D: Passed down and down; I am so tired of feeling that blackness of the heart of all wash over me and stain what I try to bring…

B: Of the good?

D: Peace that is not related to the come down after agitation, defensive, and punitive.

B: (Rubs against D and they laugh together) Our laughter is good.

D: And if we farm a circle of the living that does not trespass the cliff…

B: The cliff of reason?

D: I have longed for an understanding of this circle.

B: It is not to understand but to be in it and then everything into which it can fall off can be brought back.

D: A resumption.

B: Cherished. The horse has ridden through our fields of grass, and it no longer pauses at the river, it leaps into it, hooves flying in a specific, circumscribed pattern.

D: Who will protect you when I'm gone?

B: You can bear this circle; you do not have to leave.

D: I'm not sure, or someone isn't sure, that I'm up to it.

B: It's around, not up or down, you know that.

D: I know the size of my petals this morning and that's about it.

B: I can fit my arms around you barely.

D: Don't enchant me or we won't get to the Love that makes the circle possible.

B: I want to sit by the fireplace and watch you light a fire; I want to place my fibers up toward you and hold them to my chest in peace.

D: The timber must be around here and must be free.

B: Timber they yelled when the tree fell in the river by itself and the horse barely escaped it when pulling itself up on the other side.

D: It always seems tidy after the fact.

B: I think it's time to fill another dumpster, take the reading, take stock, then put it in the soup and sip it later when the movie is appealing.

D: And the horse got to the other side and I thought I saw it begin to gallop but that is only what I wanted, I wanted it to gallop.

B: Why? What the rush?

D: In my heart when I think of our connection, I want it now
   – be mine.

B: The possession, once she said, that he never learned that
   love wasn't possession.

D: Listening so carefully.

B: And not just because they would be tested. They wanted
   to understand their marriage in God. They wanted to
   weigh it and have it lay alongside the other one that only
   they could see.

D: And the accounts began to make sense and one didn't
   have to bring it to the other for agreement or permission
   anymore.

B: The simplicity of it. (B is stroking D)

D: Stroking, and what happened to the horse? I have a feeling
   it made it to the other side.

B: And relaxed once it did, really relaxed, like it knew that
   what it had been through was over.

D: Not that the terrain would even out exactly or be flat or
   smooth without crevice or chip, but that what was on the
   other side of the river could not cross over it again, no
   going backwards.

B: The band on the rear left leg of the horse; I saw it once; it
   was gold and narrow almost too narrow to be engraved
   or marked.

D: Once the man said he left his wedding band ajar a bit with a gap so if it got caught, it easily would snap open and wouldn't hurt his finger which he needed for surgery.

B: And you told him that it wasn't right. Close the ring for his marriage.

D: And that was the other side of the river.

B: And the broken wrist healed. There was no more honestly forgetting the scarf on the colleague's bed at the party when the coats had gone.

D: But there was a sort of normalcy in it and that was the problem. You were already in the river then, but no one knew.

B: And the horse jumped over hedge after hedge in the new land which felt familiar –

D: Looking for –

B: Faults and bridges and the warm drink.

D: The excuses did not hold water after that.

A boy on a white scooter moves by pushing off it with his left leg. He is holding nuts and screws; he is not smiling yet he looks in their direction.

B: I see that the bushes need a trim.

The time of the serious speaking ran through their entwined fibers. They took a sip of lemonade. They note the fragrance and the lilacs did not disappoint. The boy circles around to them. The boy was smart enough not to feign a smile. He did not say hello. He did not take on an apologetic stature. He stood as if saying: don't you know me? Do you see me? Do I care if you see me? They all remained silent for a moment. There was a croak, but the frogs were too far away to hear. It was an old lady at the door. She was a neighbor with a strong ear for her age. The boy loosened when he saw her, and D is pleased that the old lady let her hair come out naturally gray without an attempt to cover it over to parade an age long gone by.

The boy's shoe on the foot that he pushed off on was worn down. Age is relative, B thinks. Their fibers entwine further but know not to and how not to fuse.

Boy: What do you want with us?

D: Are you with her? She seems sweet enough.

Boy: We will water your garden for you.

D: She shouldn't work at her age.

Boy: I do the labor; she advises and predicts.

B: The storms?

Boy: The variety of possible ways of growing.

D: The time of guessing is over.

Boy: She is more surefooted; she once scaled a cliff wall.

B: With ropes, I hope.

Boy: Her fiancé was below to catch her.

D: But, let me guess, she didn't need that.

Boy: No, she didn't need it and now she is very sure.

D: What will we owe you?

Boy: Not a dime, ma'am.

D: You guessed my age.

Boy: I just spoke without guess or thought.

B: You are not a captive.

Boy: Finally, it took generations to come like that.

D: Will we take you home with us? Are you our child?

Boy: But she would have to come also.

B: She is welcome.

D: (To B) Are you sure?

B: No, but she is.

The old lady goes back inside and shuts the door. They think they hear rustling from within but are not sure and then all goes silent.

B: He is tempted to run away.

D: He has not taken my purse.

B: But all is so dry without him; you feel it too, without them both.

Boy: Stop talking about me like I'm not here – here I am.

D: Where are you from?

Boy: I am of a few countries post-virus. And she (nod to the closed door) went through them all – hot and cold wars, depression, nuclear edge that she scaled, and then it all became invisible.

D: But we see you both. Come child – (with outstretched
hand)

Boy: I am embarrassed. I am raw. I am riding away on some
other plane (he is scratching his chest).

D: We will clean you; rub you down, give you a long nap of
health and vigor.

The door opens and the old lady appears with a bag.

B: Are you Italian?

OL (Old Lady): nods no and then yes.

Boy: She is many things. I have known her most of my life.

D: Are you related?

Boy: No, but she cooks the most delicious string beans in
tomato sauce, they are delicate and soft those string
beans, they melt in your mouth.

B: She seems strong.

Boy: You're doing it again! Now you're talking about her as
if she is not here.

D: But, in all fairness, she wasn't for a long time; she wasn't
here.

OL: I went to get my bag, I'm ready now. My marriage is long
ago, and I am alone now but I am with the boy though
we hardly know one another as we truly recognize one
another.

D: The notebooks are ready to be written upon.

Boy: Are they lined with gold?

OL: Come child, we are going with them without recompense or inquiry.

Boy: Your big words…

OL: My way (she takes his arm; he walks with her with the bike on his other side); D and B walk on either side of them.

OL is walking ahead of them now.

D: Let her lead.

Boy: It's not always about us letting her.

B: Pardon?

Boy: She has her own pace.

D: Tempo.

B: Requirement.

Boy: Frame of being.

D and B look shocked glancing over the boy. Simultaneously they say: How old are you?

Boy: As old as you need me to be.

B: Is everything so malleable?

Boy: I can reach your heart.

D: (Stamps foot) Not by being so changeable.

B: (To D) We can stand it.

D: We don't know them.

B: Meanwhile, she's leading further on.

D: I want to stop at a diner. You must be hungry too.

B: (asks the Boy) Are you hungry?

Boy: I wouldn't resist food.

B: And her?

Boy: Ask her if you can.

D: Goes close to the old lady. Ma'am, are you going somewhere you have to be now? Can we stop for a bite?

OL: Of all that came before and is not.

D: What? Can you speak with me?

OL: What is the word and what the meaning and what the image?

D: We are not speaking about metaphysics. It's just a meal.

OL: Nothing that enters any body cavity is just a meal.

D: I see that actually.

OL: Seeing is relative to perception (she is leaning on her cane now).

D: I am at an angle speaking with you now, the sun is behind me.

OL: Ah, you bring up the sun.

D: It is ever in my consciousness, even at night.

OL: He was a bow and arrow.

D: She was a philosopher and mystic.

B: What's going on?

D: You tell me; we speak in what I previously would have said were riddles but now –

B: Lady, are you hungry?

OL: Depends on where of me you speak.

B: What the hell! I'm tired too.

D: Are you hungry in the soul of the space near your diaphragm?

OL: I always have been.

D: You could have told me, and you can tell me now, us now.

Boy: (Approaches D and B) I know her, and she knows me.

D: (To OL) How old is he?

OL: Of many ages depending.

B: Depending?

OL: On the grace of the Spirit.

B: Don't overlook anything.

D to B: Now you are wiser.

B: Now I have camped out enough.

Boy: So no pulling our strings.

D: You both are far too real for that.

Boy: What brought us all here beyond us? It's not enough to say synchronicity.

D: There's a father giving it over to the daughter now. Or more apt to say she took it when it was her turn.

Boy: And she is of another culture, one more Southern.

B: It's time.

OL: I am hungry in my stomach now that we've gotten there.

D: The temptations come and go but the stomach and its acids remain.

OL: We will find that diner. I will use the scent. (She taps on the earth and then smells what emanates from the connections of her wood with ground. The three watch. She lowers her head closer and closer to the earth at each tap). She stands up and smiles and says: It's a mile away.

D: A long or short mile?

OL: It's within our purview.

The OL then becomes a small, furry animal, bouncy, joyful even, a like-rabbit with patches of white and soft brown where the white looks almost pink.

Boy: (Looking at her intensely) I suppose I always have known her as such.

D: Are you sad? You lost her?

Boy: I know her better now but the other side of her is who is in my heart and cooking a lasagna.

B: You are funny.

Boy: I am safe.

D and B: Yes, you are safe.

They follow the like-rabbit who seems to be aware of them.

Aware and not aware.

The like-rabbit has a pinkish (and, of course, twitching) nose that rather matches the pinkish hue of its white fur.

This nose seems to be leading them all for the time being. The like-rabbit has not yet caught the right scent or had enough to eat that day.

The Old Lady in the boy's heart is cooking lasagna. The heart-felt.

The boy catches up to the like-rabbit and puts it in his arms. He speaks a language to it that sounds, to D and B, like Italian.

The boy sits on the edge of the grass plot. The houses are not to be seen now.

The boy hums a quiet tune. The like-rabbit relaxes. D. collects some grass and feeds it to the like-rabbit as B looks on.

I want to go home is the new phrase, but none of them knows from where it comes or what it means.

D strokes some of the soft brown and pinkish white fur as she is feeding the like-rabbit.

B still watches on, rather aloof.

Then they all sleep for a short while. Right there, on the edge of the grass all partake in the nap that has overcome the like-rabbit after having eaten.

D wakes once and looks but does not see any sort of collar on the like-rabbit's neck. The move makes the like-rabbit stir but does not wake her up.

Then D lays down with the others.

The sounds from the forest would not normally be considered as loud or disturbing.

The ferns bend to it more than from it. They had the scent for which the rabbit had searched and lent.

The ferns pick up the sound and then rustle. This rustling is an energetic breeze that enters the right ear of the boy and the most succulent cup of D.

The boy rubs his ear in his sleep. The movement wakes D and she wakes B. B goes to the boy, looks on the like-rabbit who is twitching. B touches the like-rabbit who opens its eyes and looks at B with an exquisitely fond recognition.

There is a sort of heralding here. As if a plane above had a slogan messaging off its tail but there are no words there, just the sound of a rustle from ferns long living in the ancient forest that bent to the sounds issuing forth out of it. That moment when four were sleeping at the edge of grass.

The grandmother now is in the minds of D, B, and Boy. They wish for her body, her sustenance, and her strength. They rise and walk in parallel with one another. Boy is carrying the like-rabbit. D looks up thinking a message may be there or a fading trace of one.

The boy searches in his pocket for some coins.

He finds one and puts it between his teeth: real silver, or enough silver.

He wants to get them food.

D: There will never be enough of that sort of currency to feed us.

B: Our hunger is the message in the sky for which you look.

(He starts crying which is very unusual.)

D: Hunger so vast.

B: It's the having to cook for oneself.

D: When no grandmother or human can supply.

Boy: Tyrannies.

D: The scope of it.

Boy puts down like-rabbit who starts walking and then is on two legs and it is a young woman, darker skinned.

D: But she certainly cannot be our cook.

Boy: No worries. No paranoia.

B: Paranoia?

D: What comes up when the reality as we have known it
abruptly changes and the new form is not yet visible.

Boy: When the terror can seek to be in control so sees enemy
otherwise.

D: No paranoia. But who is she? Is she the woman of your
future dreams?

Boy: She is the place of seeking connection and finds it.

B: She is wearing an off-pink skirt, that can't be good.

D: The off or the pink?

B: The vulnerable.

Boy: She will lead by following.

Some say Grazie and some say Grazia. The important
thing is to say it, most say. What triggers our striving to
balance woe and might? The hate for which we have no
appeal or recourse. In our bowels passed and stuck for eons
before wanting to dislodge.

She is speaking to them for the first time.

She: Hope is here now; the other was grasping.

Boy: So many tyrannies, so many pulls of the tendons
thought connective and perspiring.

B: Trying to breathe.

D: Cannot get out – shaking bars.

B: Resumptive. Presumptive.

Boy: Going to where one was not before.

D: Taking time.

They are breathing in unison now. They are tempted to hold hands but do not. Time reorients itself. There are bells in a distance that seems to recede. There is a clapping suggesting the show that must did go on.

Cleverness subsides more than before – going out ebbing in the waters have become polluted and they are waiting for a mighty cleansing while sunbathers flock oblivious and wanting.

They release various sighs of relief. They reach out their hands. Some crossed miles to get there. The old lady has finished cooking the dinner. She watches the TV waiting for her granddaughter to enter.

She: The food is delicious. I am hearty after it.

Boy: The earning through isolation and withstanding as well as overhauling privilege.

She: (Stands up, reaches out her hands to them) I have washed them in the unpolluted waters so the manipulations are no longer my protection from those who spike my heart. Ps 18: 1-19.

They all stand. They shake themselves as if they are shaking off water that had been sprinkled on them. A rabbit and a long-haired spaniel are lying next to one another basking in the sun which finally has lost its gender and knows who it is.

Now there is much vibrant, fervent grass around them all. B recognizes his country and is torn about returning to it or staying with this new family. Though it doesn't have to be one or the other.

She has led them to a cottage, more bungalow. There is a tiny dining room, a larger living room with a reading chair and writing table, a breakfast nook in the kitchen. They are all tense, their muscles are tight. They reverberate further. They go to the two bedrooms and find pillows and mattresses and blankets and try to get the long rest. She is awake the longest, the whirl of the mind will not calm. B comes in, sits beside her and rubs her forehead. He is undergoing a trial himself. B strokes her forehead. It is rough yet not disregarding. Then she falls into a sleep, dreaming of the tree trunk lying on the dried leaves and mushrooms with small purple buds starting to shoot. The cavity of the trunk on its side is almost dust from being so worn. A small fairy-like creature enters from the right. She is collecting fireflies and she herself has wings. She had been stationed too long in the army barracks while her mate was on leave and in the service. She is flying now, close to the earth but with wings. She still has an appetite. With the light from the fireflies, she goes further and looks into the tree's cavity. It is sumptuous though only like dust.

When the dream is over, she wakes. B is not there and there are sounds from the kitchen. The music of breakfast. Someone has gone to the market and there are eggs. She asks about the night for each of them. Not one fell into the void. She tidies herself and sits at the breakfast table with them: B and D and Boy. They hold hands in a prayer. She is really hungry. The eggs won't be enough. But they have surprised her: there is bread and some oatmeal as well. And Boy pulls from behind his back a bag of freshly made cookies. Aspiring. Sweet and salt and flour and egg and the flavors match in a soothing tone.

Don't get discouraged! They are about to fall into a slump after eating: where are they? How have they come to know one another? Is this a sort of retreat from the world they never understood? They sit in silence. It is not a crevice or cavity like the trunk had. But it is not usurping either.

There are so many times and so many ways of letting go of the false fronts.

The most difficult thing: stay with the lack. Whether silence or hole or cavity or crevice or emptiness undefined.

When the trills are seen as withered and frayed.

When the kites no longer attract.

And the family leaves one another.

There the spirits will. And the Spirit sends human buddies.

She has applauded the long offspring. She is gearing up. She sees the meaning and the forthright depth in his blue eyes. She doesn't want to reach in and sees the necessity of not even trying. Depth revealed with the screen do not enter.

The night of the long regard is over. The prison sentence is almost over and, fortunately with the mercy of God, life is not over yet. Over and done were the comedies and series of the 50's; she was teaching them a new language using those. Goodbye cell mates, here are the new buddies, all aspiring. The sun has owned finally its own rays. When they touch the vehicles, the wrapped gifts, the hearty earth blaring bouquets, there is a sizzle sound and small explosion of many colors. D is no longer called Aphrodite. B is not Icarus, or Prometheus. And the many long hours studying in the library or study rooms are done.

She is chewing and each mastication is one of the thoughts above. Her smallness regards itself. There are no more subterfuges in her own mind about what size can get through unscathed in this world.

The sound of the wind through the connecting fibers. The horses have neighed in the neighboring fields. The monetary resources are low but never quite go out.

She: What do we want from one another? Why are we together?

D: We will never know really, but just persist.

B: And have as much enjoyment as possible in it all.

Boy: Something I see, feels predetermined about it all.

She: We've gotten our rest, and the food we need, plus, importantly, the nurturance. So we go on.

Boy: Is this a Tale?

D: It's not the Head only!

B: It's the whole body and no more tensive unity.

She: Let's find what that looks like when all the parts have singularity within what we call integrity.

D: Not retaliating, telling the truth, suffering, and healing and redemption, redemptive sacrifice, repentance knowing the human limit; the cross not ballots or casino tickets or clenched fist striding leg, or worship of own willing with gods of agnosticism, colonization, industrialism, medicine and science.

Boy: Penetrating the mysteries of that Mercy.

They are at an amusement park. But their faces are rather sour. They do not attach much to that. A grape drink revives and turns their lips its color. Their hands get sticky from the cotton candy. They brush away their misgivings. They find ways out of the carriages of distrust and the sweaty clutching to subway bars. Throngs sharing sweat like in this park for amusement. Eventually their smiles resume. There are pets to keep them company that night, who knew amusement was in the park in the form of an adoption of the most forlorn of pets.

This abandonment is a strange thing.

It is yelling something to us that we cannot exactly hear. She is saying it. The Boy and D and B lend their respective ears to her. I can't hear it exactly either, but I know that a cello is involved.

And the bass, Boy says it.

I could do with an Italian coffee. That's D.

I could do with riding a motorcycle. Of course, B.

No mediation of diverse worlds this day necessary; we need a rest more even than that of the amusement park.

There is a low sigh, beyond that of the cello.

She takes them out to the meadow and they do not disapprove. They are not exactly ardent yet eager enough or perhaps that tremulous curiosity more it. They rummage through the long grass and wonder what it is she may be looking for or at. She is bent and her nose still is sharply focused. The scent alarms them when it comes, and it always comes. It is a mixture of the sweetest acidic so that acid becomes disguised. She gathers it and they ask her if it is the new drug, and would it not hurt others going for the sweet and ending up burnt.

But that is the way of the world, She smiles, and this is its antidote.

D: I thought it only could be Love, the antidote. You know that's true.

B: Yes, we have had enough of substances. Relieve us of them. We had thought more of you.

Boy: I really don't think that she is here to disappoint. Give
     her a chance.
D: It is too many degrees now; we are too hot from all the
   past of it with those we thought could be.
B: We are weary and the rest we all got will be dissipated if
   we go down the wrong path now.
Boy: Just listen.

She is standing and facing them now. She has the
substance in a bag that is a dark plastic. It had letters written
on it but that was long ago. Now it looks uniformly black and
bulging. She reaches it out to them.

D: We do not need an antidote other than Love.
She: You have spoken too much of the will in Love, you know
     that.
B: But substance? I am over those abuses.

She distributes it over the meadow while the three
remain wondrous and gasping. The old butler would have
been pleased with its evenness, the regularity of its distri-
bution. But he was eating lasagna with the grand-mother
then.

And B was the first to notice, the grass did not buckle or
cry, wither or die. He was beyond relief, for this was one of
his families of course. He lent himself to what the grass was

saying. It was speaking of leather, how the substance was some sort of protection, like leather was in the olden days.

B asks She why she wants to protect this grass, his other family, and wouldn't Love be enough?

She: It is too often understood as a card game, and who plays
with poker face and who says the words, but the heart is
not right, the heart is famished and uses tricks. This is the
acid that burns through that and which remains sweet
afterwards. That sweetness with the hint of burnt bitter
is Love.

The three sit and meditate on what She says while She is watching the substance get absorbed. The family becomes more extended. The meadow is clapping. It has learned something of encouragement to see the sweetness in surrendering to the sour, the bitter, the burning acidic without drinking it.

The meadow looks happier now, it is not hard for the three to see that.

D finds a place in the meadow which is the right one for her. The others marvel at the fit. D is surrounded by appreciation of all the blades. B is saying hello to this larger family and makes his way to D. They always have been entwined so he knows the way through the foliage of blades. They stay there quietly and speaking.

Boy and She are on the soft pavement of a sidewalk along this meadow now. They are looking at D and B. They sigh relief. Boy knows that he is being changed by this view and by standing with She. When he goes to take the hand of She, he gets rebuffed. Accept who you are, She says.

Boy is beginning to grow out of his clothes. They no longer fit him or speak his desire. That desire had been so truncated that he had almost forgotten it. It had been squeezed, fermented, and cast off in fumes. All the transgressions. But he has apologized, he has repented. He has come to help D and B. He had served the Grandmother. He had watched the movement of the sun educate gender, and he did not go under or try to surpass that.

He stands there, looking upon D and B in their place in the meadow, and he feels the groan as he moves out of his clothes. He will miss the scent of the grandmother's lasagna that had permeated them for so long.

He realizes, as the clothes drop off and he fills out: This is who we are when the father is no longer the sun and is nowhere to be found. She says: It is necessary he is nowhere now. The Boy realizes that he is no longer the Boy but he is not Father either. One glance to one another and they see the same size on many levels.

4

HAIKU

Toothpaste
Turquoise
Lime awaiting tea

Shuffling
Keyhole
Let it go

Ceramic dish
Small nick
Smiles through it

Silence entirety
Eyes intently
White fur

5

JACK
(or: If Harry/Bevel Hadn't Drowned
in "The River"[53])

Jack went to the dance, but he didn't come home with his shoes on. His grandmother would have shh-h-h-ed him, but she wasn't there. She had been fretting over the burnt porridge without quite remembering the fairy tale. The soup too was almost burnt but there it was on the stove – a film of itself veiling, waiting for him. Waiting for him to remove the veil and dig in preferably with a spoon.

It took him awhile to find the language for which he had been looking for a long while without knowing that.

First it came out almost sounding like a laugh, ha, ha. Truncated laugh, not sure of itself and certainly not enjoying itself. It was the sort of laugh that came out of not wanting to know the true moan.

For Jack was sad.

---

[53] See Flannery O'Connor's story "The River" in *A Good Man is Hard to Find and Other Stories* (NY, NY: Harvest Book, 1976), 23-46.

It was a tender underbelly of an almost ripe berry that he, in a brief glance, thought signified his heart. Not its nature but its affect. He rearranged the daisies lining the highways, crisscrossing in his mind. He thought, at first, they might be pansies but in time he reconsidered. The soup she made for him that night certainly was delicious though he bit into it more than supped. He wondered where the children had gone. He wondered who it was exactly who made such soup. The contours of his loneliness became mirrors and there seemed to be no way out.

Come through the garden child, it was the old voice still small. He picked his napkin off the floor and went out to a dusk still filled with beams. The shadows housing these beams were not disturbing nor did they intervene as he was following the voice. And so he went through the crisp marigolds and the sunbaked tomatoes and the robin toned wisps of petals here and there. There was a sort of solace in following the small voice, and the contours were no longer mirrors yet themselves the yearning.

The palpable beats of sadness. Don't run. They won't hurt. It was the embodied child once his double. The old friend of the first neighborhood. How to make up for the body unable to be embodied with a love never gotten? The absences that ugliness bearing destruction eat greedily, smacking.

The pain in his right knee called him back. What was the purpose of going through the garden after all? His mind went to reasonings. He collapsed by the shed. It had metal interwoven with wooden slabs so almost looked brick made. He caught an image as one would a butterfly. It cackled like a fire that was boisterous. He vomited at the edge of the shed. The image would not be dislodged so easily. Then the candy wrapper thrown perhaps months ago by a young unknown hand caught the eye that saw no more beams, no more shadows holding beams. No cacophony either however and for that he truly was relieved.

It was a chocolate and peanut bar once entirely wrapped and for not too many cents. Unspoken rewards – the way the chocolate coats the tongue befriending long after digestion.

The troubled path beckoned as it always must. He put the wrapper in his right jean pocket and made his way slowly in a tangential direction. Light woods, no manic defense or device, the careful wrapping of a day of mourning.

Later they might surmise the opposite. The carrier was remote enough to be a baby carriage. The food wanted to come up, but the route had been trained accordingly. Congratulations to the conductors. Empathy was not completely dead in the most directive of men.

The silences long overdue, one could say 25 years or could say culminating to it. In any event, the woods that Jack found himself within were covered with a mossy discharge (seemingly discharged) on each ample leaf. Oh, if only it had been a circus coming through town. But no blame for this grotesque. An umber green in little almost discrete lumps favoring the riper leaf. Don't destroy them he whispered passing through.

Once he thought he saw a yellow ribbon on one of the branches. He searched his mind for what that could mean. Boys at war? The plague? He thought of cowardice in his own life and that of close others. He threw off the blanket that had invisibly combined with his upper back for decades. It was hardly worn, but tired nonetheless of the role. His right ankle rolled over once, and he examined the bark right there that looked like it had white chalk writing on it. Or was it a picture? He drew closer. He watched the magnitude of his feelings teeming through every limb. Limber. Limp. His ankle revived as he saw the drawing: a circle with a moose head inside. Emblem of what he thought once was strength.

What the intention of this animal? More to the point, what was he himself doing in this wood anyway? Could the vastness of his sadness ever find relief in bark and chalk antler? His foot almost landed in a hidden, slight crevice. He backed away from the tree. He did not want to land in excrement of any form. He tired of the moss, the chalk, the moose in thirty seconds. He wanted out of these woods. He wanted the refreshing tone of splashes inside and out – movement, fluidities in sparkle and bubble and spray.

It was so stationary, so static here. Almost. Twigs tore beneath his soles. Brief decisions whether to go unshod. He thought of the cowboys and their boots. Some had heels. He thought of the actresses on their stilettos and those that refused to balance accordingly.

It was so stationary. He wanted to reach to the sky to cry, cry for, cry out. But even that was more ceiling. Cerulean. Cerealian. Celiac. Please, he called out, and yes, it was upward. Where is my Angel? He heard the words and knew they were his own, yet he did not quite understand them.

The walls were not listening. The walls were talking amongst themselves. So he was able to slip through.

He wondered, as he walked through the lighter brush, what the moose would be saying. Some memory of a train was following him, and he pushed on. Is the Moose my Angel? He was saying it aloud still. No, he knew, though he sought companionship, was desperate for it, he knew that Moose was a sign to gather courage and carry on. Slowly, like an elephant. The Moose brought him to think of the elephant. The one that got out of the center of the boa constrictor, after all.

So he lumbered along, slowly, as if dragging a trunk. He was surprised when he looked straight ahead and there was a line. The woods came to an end in a horizontal line of trees. Just like that; though it had taken so much time to get there. He paused before this line as if he had a decision to make. What pushed him over, it was more of a prompt. The sort of nudge that one only realized as such years later. The detectives were removed from the scene. The evidence was compromised. So he crossed the line of trees.

There was the inevitable road, with the bars of sunlight gracing it just before dusk. There had been maneuvers on it during the day, cars posturing, gestures signifying, not just people in cars going on their way but some in promenade: to show oneself off in order to feel one as being. The ignitions turned in any event.

The time of the turntables was over. He looked at various scratches on his hands. He turned over the dying rose that he forgot he was still clasping. It had made it through the forest with him. He wondered if it wanted to go further or just be left in a habitat more hospitable to its nature. He was sorting through signification in his back mind but then, with hope of it never becoming regret, placed the dry rose by the extended, visible roots of the maple tree.

He was about to step onto the road, but, deciding against that, walked alongside it. He was being kissed by the dropping rays of the sun, so he looked right at it and asked if it was hungry. The rays hugged him further as if they were grateful for his inquiry mounting care. His hands were empty now and were flapping at his side as he walked the roadside. It felt like being in a wry cowboy movie, walking off but not in the sunset, in front of it.

When he got to the tavern, it was fully night though he could see wisps of clouds from the streetlights. The door opened as some people were leaving and the daze of alcohol encased in the warm rust of air almost threw him off. Off from whatever path it was to be. Certainty was a mere whiff itself. But some circuit regained him and, back on it, he countered the rust air and went in.

Hail and laughter back slapping mouth open guffaw and this was a new sort of womb, one into which he would not have chosen to submit or condescend before his time in the woods.

The plank on the ship for pirates was not necessary for a long while, but, in a strange way, he wished he had one now. Sons of justice. And where was she? He saw stairs going up by the far wall. He went to the bar. It was all like looking at a magazine cover in a supermarket. Flashes of masks. He asked for a ginger and rye. It sounded good coming out of his lips; it had been very long since he actually had spoken words to anyone. They came out like tinsel being stripped off a beyond-its-date Christmas tree showering dried needles at a breeze's touch.

The bartender was thirty and a woman who looked tired and that more than just her hair had been dyed. There was something decidedly artificial about her, but he almost had a sense, furtively studying her further, that someone was trying to get out of there. Was this the "she" about whom he had asked? Where is she?

The torrents of rain began when he was considering whether to order another drink. Now he had to stay there. He asked for a room. There were two left. He took the one that he was told was in the back. Where are you from? It was not the artificial woman who asked but a man coming to take over, to take the shift. He had a belly becoming pot that it seemed he liked to exaggerate, given the tight t-shirt and its whiteness. From beyond Montana way, Jack replied. Next question: From the hills? Yes, and canyons, and then the woods.

Want to be mystery man, huh? It came out like a dare more than a threat.

I don't want to get in any trouble mister. He said it in a voice imitating the old cowboy movie characters, he said it like a joke.

She laughed first and that eased things. He recognized for a moment who was trying to get out of her. It was not that the atmosphere lightened, but definitely changed hue. Jack took the key and went upstairs. No one followed him, not even with a glance, but he suspected that he would be the subject of laughter and critique and that did not annoy him.

The door of what now is his room opened to a slight smell of lavender. It was not a strained smell and it quivered through the room. The door opened to a double bed with a worn cotton woven spread, an oak dresser, and a small bathroom. Sparse and tidy while perfectly compensating for the thick woods. The door opened to a woman's voice, almost that of a child: do you have a penny, sir?

He swiftly turned around. No one there, the hall resounded an emptiness preferring that. He then quickly searched his room, beneath the bed, behind the shower curtain. No trace of the origin of that question. He heard it again: Do you have a penny, sir?

He smiled, thinking of the after-effects of the wood and of the reasons why he had entered it. Such experiences must give off certain vibrations and this sound was one. He sat on the bottom of the bed and slowly edged off his boots. The mud caked and sour sock smells entranced him, almost imploring him, to go back to that place of grudge, sweat, and that strange unfamiliar might. It was so tame here. So utterly human. He was in a disguise, he thought. Not that he was disguised, or was the disguise, but he was right then and there sitting in a disguise.

He listened for her again. It did seem to come from the bathroom. He made his way there barefooted. The wooden floor gave way to spotted tile with pock marks. He looked up and above the tub was a ceiling with a yawning brown spot, a ceiling needing repair. But she did not come from that.

He went back into the room and opened the top drawer of the dresser. A woman had been there, again a smell spoke. He touched the plywood base of the drawer, what it had felt: he touched what it had felt. He enjoyed these new sensations. He took a penny out of his wallet. He placed it on the plywood and shut the drawer.

The time of the dance was over. The customers were shuffling to their own homes. The masks they had taken off were swept up and the bartender went home to his own bed.

Jack spent some of the night looking for signs of her around the room. He couldn't locate her smell anywhere else, nor could he hear another question or word; at one point, he thought he felt her touch when he was in the bed. He thought he felt her hand on his shoulder, moving down gently to his elbow. He hadn't remembered her that tender before. He suppressed an urge to push her arm away and leave the bed himself.

When he saw the Angel there was no irony in any part of the atmosphere. He relished the thought but then saw that it was no thought, was no part of his doing, his thinking, or even his intention. All he could do was to wonder about her relation to the other her, the one whose arm he had wanted to push away.

When he saw the Angel, there was an absence of doubt that really surprised him. Where is the doubt? Where does it go in such a split-second moment? Is it like moving swiftly from NY to San Francisco? He smiled that this was his first thought. When he saw how attentive he was being to his mental response to the Angel, he realized that he was not attending to her.

Very early that morning, he looked to where he had seen her. The moon facing him through the window was waning. Angel and wane and where is the mother in between? He couldn't stop thinking it through.

He lay back down on the bed, hands over eyes. He tried to find her there in the dark of each palm. He gulped as if he were under water. He felt as though he was sinking. Then he flooded up as his body told him it was not the time to go under, not the time to stay under. The Angel had been who long ago had lifted him in the river, after the Angel had fought off the molester.

Beliefs are everywhere. The molester had believed in the Devil. The Angel put the Molester to shame, and the molester finally stopped following the Devil, and Jack did not die then. So now Jack again can come out of the river. He took his hands off his eyes, he sat again at the edge of the bed, and he put on his boots. The mud caking them had hardened to a degree that now it looked like leather. But leather was not mud.

He went to the small sink in the bathroom and washed his face. His mask came off with some scrubbing. It looked like soft plastic as it folded on the porcelain of the sink. He stared at it for a long while, both wishing it would dissolve down the drain and fearful that it would since he might have to reuse it.

He thought he heard a dog panting behind his door. His first thought was a question to himself: Does the Angel take shapes? He looked around the room again, looking for her. Without a mask on, he could see everything in more detail. Colors seemed more animated as well. He clutched at his belt, calmed by the surety of leather. She was nowhere to be seen or heard, but he sensed that she was there. He went to open the door.

The panting dog was there. Where is your owner, buddy? A boy about 10 years old came running around the rear corner of the hall. When the boy saw the dog, he exclaimed: Tommy! The embrace was followed by the reprimand followed by another embrace. The boy scolded the dog for running off his leash. The parent from two doors down reprimanded the boy for not holding onto the leash better and then reprimanded the dog.

Jack stood as a calming presence amid it all. He was breathing evenly while realizing that the mask had dissolved down the drain when the Angel had come, and that realization registered as evenness on his face. The boy noticed it. The boy smiled at him, thanked him for finding his dog. But I didn't find him, Jack replied, rather he sort of found me; he was at my door, perhaps he thought it was yours.

The boy's mother came and took the leash. There was to be no confusion of doors. She had a sharp step and a bewildered look that was benevolent enough. She's just being careful, Jack thought. Mother and son and dog walked back to their room two doors down. What would such people be doing rooming over a bar? Jack wondered. He pulled his pants further up and tightened his belt. He went back into his room. Though no scent of the Angel was apparent, Jack sensed that the dog had sensed the Angel.

Later that day, he was having a beer at a small round table in the bar, and it was the mother who came over. She had been eating there with another woman who left the bar as the mother approached Jack. He collected his wallet and the change that he had dropped on the table to make room for her. But she remained standing over him. He felt a small shock go down his spine. Was she a drinker like his mother had been? Was she someone who frequented bars? Is this why the boy lost his grip on the leash? But those thoughts were not the shock. The shock was in her glance. It had a look or warnings of sorts: don't go near my boy or else.

I'm not that sort of fellow ma'am, he fired back at her with his own glance upwards. I was at the other end of that, and I have not, I repeat, I have not become it. I do not fend off or retaliate against my own past in those ways. Would you like to sit down? he said aloud.

I just want to clear up any misunderstandings, she replied. So you weren't going to let the dog in and keep it? He heard the word dog but knew she meant son. No ma'am, I've no need of a dog, I'm not a drifter, ma'am.

She clicked away in her sharp step. He fingered his glass. He smiled but, without the mask, he knew she had gotten through, and he was hurt, he felt hurt, ashamed, the old shame for no reason.

He sat there alone for another hour. What is your message now? he asked the Angel. You are too alone, came the reply, and, it continued, that is the repetitious remnant of the alcoholic, drug infested, poverty ridden rooms of your childhood. Those ashes were rubbed into the rug long ago. Get up, get out.

That night, the attack of insomnia came reinforcing, in a clipped, definite way, what he had heard at the table. Get up, get out. So he did. From behind, it looked like a car going off alone down a long road with not many clouds in a sky just beginning to redden. From behind. But he was trying to look forward. Look forward to what? How to look into a blank while driving down the road only known as some road? It didn't matter, though it may have if he had a goal, if he knew to what to look forward. For now, it was a matter of just getting out.

He thought of tightening his belt again, but kept driving, wanting the space to let out air, to let go. It was the time before most woke. He had been driving through the night. He veered off and stopped at an eating place that looked like a cabin, a log cabin. It was all for show but it did calm him.

He pulled up to the door to see when it would open, and he saw a light on, so he parked and went up to the door. The screen in front was torn in two places but that seemed fine by him. Things happen, he thought, kids run around with play swords and fairy wands. Kids don't mind the screens of life; they go right through them. He thought he saw a piece of mauve cotton caught in the screen. He thought it might be from a girl's skirt. He wondered if the girl had noticed. Did anyone notice her torn skirt? Was it an embarrassment or a token of courage? He wiped his nose. The screen came open easily enough, but the sign said Opening 6am and the door was locked.

He would have to wait forty-five minutes. He felt his tiredness, bone tiredness. He knew no doctor could minister to that. It was in the heart's core, this tiredness. He stumbled on some loose stones as he went back down the steps, and this is when he heard the door opening and the screen creaking its own movement. He almost didn't look around; the urge was to get to the accelerator with a right foot and press hard. Instead, he sat down on the step, which even he thought was a strange response. He didn't even look around.

He sat and looked over the terrain looking more like a desert laced with nostalgia. He sat as the steps came closer and descended to what was not his seat. She had on an apron that smelled of bacon fat and burnt toast. Her hair looked stringy and desirous of many washings. Altogether, her drawn skin, her bandaged finger, her half-lit eyes, her loyal, worn-out boots, and her snide glance indicated a great need for a warm bath and the touch that could soothe by searing years of neglect. He wanted to do that for her. He had nothing else to do and nothing else to offer.

Jack leaned back on both elbows, so now he was taking up two steps. He did not want to look at her anymore, so he just took to listening. He heard the early morning dove; he heard the bear in the far-off wilderness rubbing his hide in the dried leaves. He listened for the Angel. He knew she was there but also that she was not related to this woman sitting on the step to his right.

He wanted to put something in his mouth to relax into the moment. He picked some blades of grass along the side of the steps and put them in his mouth as if he was that old cowboy after all.

"Romans 13:11. It is full time now for you to wake from sleep." He heard it clearly; it was coming from the one to his right on the step. He responded automatically without the glimmer of a thought and said: But I haven't even slept all night. He hadn't been that literal for a long while.

She was looking at him now. She could see that the mask was off, and she was surprised he was being so literal. We are all sleeping, she responded tentatively.

A long silence, to which he stayed close, followed.

The time of sleeping like dinosaurs is over, she said, less tentatively. He pulled two more large blades of grass and began to chew on them.

I've had enough with cigarettes myself, she said, I've had many packets and the smoke hurt my eyes. Blades of grass makes more sense; plant-based diet, she laughed.

She had on a maroon tank top. He looked at the tattoo on her upper arm. It was a flower with pink and orange alternating petals. In its center, it said: NONE.

He said it aloud as he was looking at it: NONE. He wanted to put his forefinger right there, indent it. Then there would be something, not none. She had the look somewhat of his mother, so he was cautious. Yet his mother, even in her better days, would not have had the self-awareness to signify NONE.

Are you a city boy now a cowboy on the road? It was a simple enough question and she asked it without sarcasm. She asked it deliberately and more as an open-ended inquiry and not just to pass the time. She was curious about him.

There was nothing left in him but to tell the truth. An Angel, no, my Angel, pulled me out of a river when I was a very young boy and almost drowned, when I was in there looking for the Kingdom of God. I almost drowned then in my self-made second baptism. Back then she lifted me out. I felt and heard her recently and that brought me through the wood and to a hotel over a bar and to another escape.

Man, she said, I feel like offering you an ice cream or something – no kidding – you're not kidding, are you?

It's all true. It's me waking up. You said: time for all to wake up.

Who is the Angel?

I'm finding it out.

So I have one. Where is mine?

It's part of what Christ left us, the Advocate, remember? You know the Bible, you quoted it earlier.

Holy Spirit, she said as she threw out her legs in front of her. They were shapely in her cropped shorts and very much suggesting availability until the boots which said stop.

She continued: He'd leave us the Holy Spirit, yes, man, He has done that, but sometimes I don't see it much anywhere, sometimes even not much around here, but it's here and folks know it underneath it all.

It's your Angel that is the way to it. That's what He meant: the Holy Spirit works through each of our Angels, but to find her we have to clear all the debris, the mess, in our bodies, in our hearts and the mind of our hearts and know ourselves. That's my journey now, through the woods on.

You being a smart-ass fellow?

No, I can tell you are a Bible person, and you are following me, don't pretend you're not.

OK, I got to get the grits on. I own this place. The folks will be coming for their coffee and morning hello talking soon. She stood up and nodded her head to him and went inside.

He threw out the chewed blades and sat there wondering what next. Where was that Angel now?

He remembered a scene: his cousins were play acting the balcony scene in Romeo and Juliet and one threw the other off an actual upper staircase while saying Romeo, Romeo, where are you? Here I is! replied the one thrown into the air. And another caught him on the way down.

Jack, sitting on the steps of the eating dive said: Here I is.

He smelled the bacon more poignantly. She had left the door open. He went in.

If only I could just state by my presence: Here I is. He sat at a table by the window instead of at the counter. He thought of the Bible again; he thought of "Jesus wept". Does his Angel weep?

The owner woman brought him out a porcelain mug of coffee and cream in plastic containers. The sugar's on the table, she said in her low voice, if you take that.

How come you know the Bible? He asked it quietly.

We do around here, and I made a special look at it when I lost my second child.

Sorry, so sorry.

It's all part of it mister. She looked for the first time into his eyes and then turned to return to her grill.

The hardened workers came or more shuffled in shortly afterwards. Worn clothes but clean and comfortable; scruffy beards mostly graying; heavy, stocky frames though not fat or soft, very tough skins in fact.

The Angels are all around these folks, he thought, but he couldn't place his yet, didn't even exactly know if his was a he or she.

Coffee disengaged from the pot readily; the grits flowed through the tables. Someone sat without eating and was thinner than the rest. He was rather scrawny, in fact, though he seemed to Jack to be generous in spirit. Jack wasn't sure how he thought that, or why, but when he finished his coffee, he left a large tip on the table and walked over to the man.

He could hear the owner woman talking with laughter with those at the counter. He could hear her engaged in a farm story about a cultivator that went backwards. The laughter from the counter seemed strange so early in the morning but he figured that it was natural for these folks.

As he approached the thinner man, the man looked up. His eyes once had a sparkle that was slowly departing them. The sparkle once there caught Jack's attention. This man's Angel is retrieving it, he thought, and he smiled deeply, inwardly at that thought.

He asked the man if he could sit down. The man looked surprised, almost a shock flashed across his face, but he quickly regained himself. He put out his right open palm pointing to the seat across from him.

The man's eyes were a clear blue, almost cobalt. Jack disengaged from them when the owner woman came to the table asking the man if he wanted anything more and Jack if he wanted anything at all.

Another Bible verse would be great, Jack replied, surprising himself, but not surprising, he noticed, the man sitting across from him.

"I will raise up shepherds over them who will shepherd them, and they shall not fear any longer, or be dismayed, nor shall any be missing, says the Lord."

The thinner man added: a Righteous Branch will grow from the stump of David.

That comes right after the Jeremiah 23:4 verse in NRSV that I said, she explained.

Wow, Jack said, you people are educated in the Bible.

That's all the education we need for us around here, she threw out as she departed and went to a conversation at the adjacent table. Jack decided not to eavesdrop there and to focus on the one before him.

So, I saw you sitting here, and I was alone too, so I thought I'd come over since I just arrived in these parts and don't know about them.

Farming, mostly. I know it looks like a desert some around here but further out a couple of miles the farmland is quite good particularly this year since we've had a lot of rain, thank God.

God is over your folks mightily; I can see that.

Yes sir. We farm and we cultivate and harvest as we await the Age of the Spirit. It's upon us now.

I once heard a preacher by a river speak of Jesus in the way you do here. He was baptizing and bringing others to Jesus and the Kingdom of God. A woman who was taking care of me brought me to Jesus and to that preacher. Yes, I think I know what you mean.

You been away from the Book and Church for a bit?

Jack replied with a half a laugh, as if mocking himself: Yeh, you could say that. After almost drowning in that river, I went up North and went to schools and a good job but then missed that river and came back here and saw my grandma, not of blood, I never knew that one, but of life, the woman who gave me Jesus, and yet I had to go through some woods and the wrong town before I was sure I wanted to come back to it all and wanted to clear out myself to do so.

Come back to it all? Here were raised eyebrows over the thin, narrow face.

The land, the Book, that way of seeing, of living.

Yeh, I see.

And it seemed to Jack that the thinner man actually did see. There was something about this man that seemed both preternatural and innate.

We know the Book here, the man continued, as part of the Church Sacraments, no divisions. The Sacraments need the Book like the Book needs the Sacraments. Come to the Mass for Sacraments and no river will drown.

Jack sighed.

It's hard, huh? The man seemed sincere.

Big changes. Excuse me for just coming out with it like this but: also, I'm following my Angel who got me here.

I gotcha, I do.

Jack looked surprised, but, when he thought about it, he wasn't.

A man passing their table was saying something to Jack who could barely understand a word of it since the accent was very thick and the man spoke fast. The thinner man translated: they deliver corn in burlap sacks like in the olden days, if you want any.

Jack looked at the incomprehensible one passing by who now had paused at their table and said to him: No need right now, though I may stay around these parts. No saying now, I just rode in, so to speak.

The passing man uttered a short laugh and, saying welcome, left.

Now Jack laughed.

The thinner man said: their farm's corn really is good, the kind of sweet that's not too, you know, mushy sweet.

I'll definitely consider those sacks if I stay.

The owner woman came back with a full coffee pot and no words this time expecting that her gesture would state the obvious.

The thinner man told her that he was done for the morning, and then told her, nodding to Jack, that the stranger may stay around.

You're welcome to do that, she said to Jack, even with your accent. You don't need no river to find that kingdom you know.

The world has changed, Jack said, looking down in his empty cup.

But, she added, the Holy Spirit is not in all that kooky stuff that forgot Jesus either.

The thinner man said to her: He's finding his Angel going to Spirit. He's got Jesus in his blood and that's what matters. A woman long ago gave him Jesus and he mistook it at first, but she had put Jesus in his blood. Jesus been carrying him through the North, the wood, to the wrong town, and to here. You're part of this town, mister.

With no initiation? He said it almost as a joke and regretted it as soon as it was out.

She walked off. The thinner man got up, took both the checks on the table saying he would take care of them and that it was really good to meet.

Finally, Jack said into his cup, finally.

He remembered what he had book learned up North: feeling like a stranger is the same as wanting to return home when home is the celestial on earth and the celestial is able to be seen within and through the earth, because one has cleared out, through suffering, the impediments. The Book and the Sacraments were calling him back.

He thought: The Angel is my guide in this way of the return. I know that, but what next?

The owner woman passed by him again and looking at him smiled while moving on.

He sat in his car outside the grill place. He didn't want to look into getting a room. He had had enough of them from dorms on: the bed in center, the scarred basin, the rutted dresser. Sometimes a frayed rug when he preferred the tenacity of the wood alone.

Yet he also had had enough of the woods and that peculiar, particular darkness; he had earned his way through it and really did not want to return.

He recalled, as he often did, the translucent image of the peppermint stick that the craven devil man had had as a lure, long ago, twenty-five years ago. No, it was not about going back.

If no room, then what? He had bought a small cherry tart, the packaged sticky kind, at the gasoline station on the main road. He ate a bite and licked his fingers. He looked at them and asked: are you still greedy to make up for being so mistreated early on – they're gone, all those people are gone now – can you possibly relax into the task at hand and help me to get a place, some roots planted?

He continued: everything now further will be cleansed, his diet, his thought, his desiring and despairing heart, the mirror of his heart, to stay with his Angel. And by now he knew it would take more than an act of will.

He was talking to his Angel without knowing it at the time.

Why not a farm area, perfect for planting roots.

Now I'm talking to my hands, he thought, yet whom am I really addressing? Where are you Angel? You helped to get me this far. Where are you now, today, this very minute?

He sat in the silence that did not hover oppressively. He sat and wiped the rest of the sugary hardening film off his fingers.

Better yet: who are you?

It came clearer than the daylight that he was sitting within: I am your other side, celestial other side that you will be when more of God and thereby your true vocation.

I had vocations, he thought, then said out loud.

But there are different aspects of vocation throughout life that feel like changing jobs, but then there is the last one, which you are approaching now, which is their integration and culmination.

Like the rest were practice as I got, suffering them, burning them off, to you?

Yes, celestial twin.

He put his forehead on the steering wheel. It was almost too much to take. But not too much.

I'm ready, he thought, I'm finally meeting you.

He started his car and went to the first realty building he saw. He sat across the desk from two people who sorted through rented homes for him.

The one he chose was small and modern and mostly furnished. Two stories. A lot of wood inside it – wood paneling, floors, and furniture. He needed a dog.

The pound was howling. Half shepherd, half something else. He called her Time.

He cleaned and fumigated the place. Time ate. He put a quilted spread over the couch. He had found it in the attic space, in a chest, and had aired it out all afternoon.

The fireplace hadn't been used for a long while. He cleaned and scraped it out. He went back to the grill place, and she was in there, cleaning up.

She knew about chimney cleaners. She knew where to go for one. That was a task for tomorrow, for the next day.

6

The Blackboard (sob heard)

The corner, the 90-degree angle of the two stone walls, in tepid soil, was where she crouched. Her fear of God no longer rested on that person or some person. She was holding the rope woven by the friend of her uncle. It had a small, red metallic bell at one end. She is wondering: If I ring it, will the cows come home? She knew the thought was part of a wound, the one in the shape of the crucifix.

For a brief time, she wished she could rely on high and mighty to defend against not only the wound but its suppuration. She realized that she could not feel the wall on every part of her back since she was sitting in the corner. Yet it suited her. It suited wound and well-being being in this corner. To be and sit in corner as agent not patient.

To have the patience to sit in the corner as agent. The various creeds required it. The red skin was suppurating once. The creed was salve. Her mental capacities. She breathed in so far it almost became snort. The sound enough to fend or scare though that was not her intent as agent.

She required the back rub and the two ends where the two walls lined her back was enough. Her spine could not reach the spine of the corner, but spines of book are not useless. It was not to be a wall of support, more leaning to it.

Up and down, the breathing relaxed into itself. The puff from the old breath terminated in an oval cloud in the cooling air. As if she was smoking and blew the evanescent silver tiny ball.

She stood up and it was like standing in a hot tub. Once she had been invited in. Declining like drifting, in vision down the sandy slope wanting moisture but knowing better.

All mooring gone. The wrist band was too worn. She snapped it off. Her demeanor had hardened, she had another tale to tell. The sumptuous feast leaving one whispering to oneself with forefinger on lip: it needs something, but not necessarily spice or herb.

The ramshackle cobblestones leading outside the garden, clomp clomp, the clogs on cobblestones as if she were in another age subtracting hundreds. She bent to stroke a small wildflower that managed to peak through the earth crack combining stones. There was hardly anyone left. She no longer hijacked. She no longer needed a scarf. What of those who said love yet harbored malevolence. There was no protection of the neck then.

The balloons shot up and crisscrossed against the blue-gray sky, an attempt, not necessarily futile, to cheer it up. This sky was sad. It had lost potency as it watched the cobblestone remain, yet the years increase. It had lost lining and substance and a referral for justice. At times it wanted the medieval firmament back. It hastened for a recovery and understanding. It was so blank, indeterminate, and uncertain in this accumulating impotence.

The high school girls were playing field hockey as if it was true. Knees banged more than the rackets. The time of supposition was over and done. They no longer drank milk suspected curdle. One wrote in her journal that night about winning that had been a surprise. She was a target of someone then when playing, she saw it in the eyes. She thought they were in a dance but now she saw that was a front. Winning was insignificant after all.

Showering cascade and she was washed. Who can understand the exact timing of such? The balloons, no longer necessary, went their own way. The old leather chairs looked twin and the creases on them magnified their wear. She had entered the den open to whatever wanted her eye. Her right eye, the eye that was determined as she could be. From the start.

The one who was human who met her came out from the back of the creased dark brown almost maroon leather chair. He may have been writing on the back of it since he had a pencil in his right hand, waving it as if truce, as if a stunned soldier who no longer knew or appreciated his aim.

The deviations from the walk, or bypass, or derivations.

But she greeted the boy as though there was no deviated aim, no stunned wandering step. She greeted him as though he was just a boy at play yet beneath her grin and her outstretched arms, she told him in no uncertain, unheard words that she knew the battle that encompassed his being. She knew it as if she had been every minute there. She knew it so intimately that there never could be a doubt. And he got the message and was soothed.

So he gave her the pencil and trotted away. The ones in the other rooms continued as if he was a boy who had not been in a battle, as if he was an unencumbered-by-battle boy. He went along with it for the sake of some semblance of home, of what some call security. Only decades later would he finally realize that those rooms had to be burnt in his midriff and only find place in weathered and remembered albums stored in mental drawers.

She heard him in those other rooms, and she sat on one of the leather chairs. She put her legs out and looked them over. They needed a rest, from the field hockey, from the lonely sky, from the cracks between and often within the cobblestones calling forth foot forward do not doubt.

The tremors ran like blue tendrils within her body from neck to toe. It was not a joke. It was the foresight of something of which she could not be completely sure. The tissue on the side table caught her sneeze easily. Then, crumbled on the broad arm of the leather chair, it suggested rose bud disengaging from its bind and just now feeling its way out, happy, hopeful, and where the sharp contrast of light and shadow made way for the suggestion of halted movement, a taking a breath in the midst of rapid, thrilling, tremulous growth.

Then she stood up and went into the rooms to have a drink with the others. To say hello and recount the happenings since last engaged. To be cheery and uplifting as offering of heart to whom she could not herself relate. Those rooms, later to be burnt in midriff and saved in the drawer, those rooms were what make the worldly work. They are not to be criticized or deemed unworthy. They hold up the structures of who society thinks it is and has to be. They are history and standard and convention and are part of the slow trotting necessity.

One there wanted to take her out.

He had a shawl around his neck as scarf. She thought of the waiters with towel over arm to catch the drip. Would he wait for her? Was she worth waiting for? Would he catch the drift? Is she worth it? She touched the strand of pearls at her throat. She ran the tips of her fingers over them twice. She caught the drift. The ocean resumed its cadence. It had been in the storm, it had been an ingredient in said storm and now the culmination, the feast, that which comes from it all, not necessarily personal design but the full pleasure of it. An even easygoing rhythm. Lulling as stimulating in the precise hold of that polarity. That was their conversation. She didn't know what could come of it. Even later, she never was sure of what did come of it.

She excused herself from speaking with him and went to the table and took an orange from the fruit bowl. The fruit was coarse in its skin and felt an easy contrast to pearl. She went back to him, still holding it. It was a sudden decision to move away and come back to thwart the grief beginning to well within the conversation. No rough tide, no storm, just the simple flow of it between them and that was frightening.

The lightning that may have begun between them disappeared, without thunder. Certainly, no applause. She put down the orange after he refused a piece of it. His scarf was striped and caught the shine from overhead lighting the heads of those thinking they belonged in such rooms. She gave him the grieving instead of the orange. This he could not refuse.

They set a date for an excursion. The moors were waiting for them. The moors were ripe. The ribbon candy of the season looked so delicate but the chips when broken could be very sharp.

They both had on the required tweed and walked slowly up the scree. She looked for stream but there was no water anywhere. She was disappointed. She wanted fresh water not just the grieving, she wanted fresh water and for the land to give back to her all that she had lost.

He played the rampart, he played the toy soldier, the delicate harlequin, the puppet with the fixed, unerring smile. He had been beyond-lonely spending so much time in those rooms that he no longer recognized the need or who he could be on the moors with her.

He stopped playing. They stopped walking. He could not look at her. He looked down onto the dry ground. He let the aching parchment in his gut be known. She saw and recognized it. It was like it could catch fire at any moment but that was not to be. That would be too easy. That was the usual way. She saw it remaining dry, so parched, and painful. The gentleness of the pain indeed was disarming.

No family. And which to start. How to start.

She was tempted to enchant him. She fought it by non-resisting. It flew in and out. Let it go, she had caught that disease and the antibodies finally worked. She better could handle when she was mistreated by anyone and was more conscious of her previously unaware, unintentional mis-treatment of another.

So she was allowed to see the parchment and it did hurt. They took one another's hands. They decided to walk to the closer village. Small, shops, places to sit that were patient with longer conversation. The quaintness had an appeal. It soothed.

Heavy competition arises from the edge of the parch-ment when neither enter the fullness of the ache. So now they no longer were competing. The orange from their meeting long had been eaten by a stranger.

Who is the monster in each of us attracted to itself? He asked.

The words came readily from her: monster is raging of course and reliably so. It has a curled down left bottom lip. It craves sugar, molasses, over-ripe fruit; it sees genital primarily as pounding to pulp pleasure. It is uncannily incestuously minded without knowing it. Its pounding also is waves in frontal cortex that misconstrues, projects, suspects, condemns self and others.

And we, he added, have served others to compensate for our secret unconscious knowledge of monster, as if to hide it further from ourselves and all others.

In the village, they could look at one another, sitting across.

What was the orange about? He asked serenely.

I thought it was to relieve us both of the intensity of our encounter. It was the first thing I saw on the table, so I grabbed it. It felt coarse in my hand, yet the inherent juice was consoling.

Was it an offering to you or from you to me?

More a propitiation, now I think, of the monster between us. The monster of each of us that attracted one another, and the grieving behind that.

He said: I was thinking of looking perplexed just now but actually I'm not.

He offered his hand.

Not until we know these two monsters.

Are they not the same – is that not why we were drawn to one another?

Yes and No. I don't know, but I know they resonate with one another. I had avoided mine for ages, she added, instead took on or let others apply their monsters to me in order not fully to know mine. I have had glimpses of it and one strong look which showed me hell and sent me back to Church and Spiritual Protection.

He said, I was in seminary once.

Why did you leave?

I saw or was shown how I have the tools that I was given there, learned there, to keep me from being overtaken by monster yet it was not my vocation to stay there.

Yes, she replied, I know them now too, finally, the tools to work through the monsters without destruction, tyranny, or vice.

His serenity enveloped her and there was no stamp that said he was leaving, being posted elsewhere yet more would stay posted.

Trust comes hard after letting others' monsters dominate in order to appease and humiliate one's own, she said it clearly.

But what inner illnesses!

Of course.

So, monster to monster they met over the table in the village coffee shoppe.

If only the monsters could shake hands and call it a day, she said. But instead: irritability when it claws to get out, and, depending on transmission history and temperament, sadism of various degrees from microaggressions to slander to frontal attack.

They paid and went for a stroll in the village.

They both found that they were each completely congested.

Appeal of cracked vessels after the monsters did their due.

The charity when we each took on the monster raging in the family, tumultuous forces surging through caregivers, we took that monster on to relieve the ones we loved. Or was it duty.

He replied: Monster comes because it has no family and has lived too long isolated, so it tears through the family.

They were walking side by side on the stone sidewalk. She remembered the cobblestones, the crack there, the stretching stem appealing, supplicating, through the crack, and she wanted to take his hand.

They were walking side by side on the stone sidewalk and, in her mind and perhaps his, holding hands.

They came to the candy store with the peppermint stick candy cane, large though not imposing, in the front window. Sweet shoppe. She rubbed her gray pearl necklace lying close to her throat. She could take some sweetness going down it, this throat. The edge of parchment was wearing away. It went by the words that they were speaking to one another as they were holding hands in imagination.

This throat let out the silent words: do not neglect the negligee, the delicate fabric seeing through. See through the peppermint stick: no quick stimulate orient to white to red; no easy passage from white to red. Monster cannot be ignored. Monster strips through it all. They are looking inside the window. Monster does not abide negligee. It does not want to see through. It wants, it needs, to gobble. It wants to have esophagus be touched bam. It has been afraid of its caverns. They have exploded so often, and others thought it him.

Monster whispers to her inner ear while she is standing beside him. They thought it me, but the explosion was through me due to my fear of the caverns there alone in them that had become too familiar and terrifying. When I went off then you broke into parts.

And the part with this man here now, right here? she asks monster, quietly, slowly.

That is of the chest. But not yet the heart.

But not yet the heart, she repeats. She asks monster: Can it ever be of the heart and not just stimulant infatuate when there are still the parts? Can there ever be anything called harmonious relationship of the heart when one is in all in pieces to various degrees? It is not enough to say that the parts dialogue with one another and that joins, conjoins.

Now the man beside her, the man who saw her get the orange that some stranger later would eat, that man is speaking as if he heard the entire interchange between her and monster. He is saying: it is not enough to say that love heals monster though that is a help, but the problem is that the one we fall in love with has a monster too, attracted to ours, and eventually they both emerge in power dilemma, competition, destruction. The parchment ache goes under, and the monster power dilemmas take over.

They have gotten to a small park with a swing set. Three children are swinging and sliding and are joyful. Then the children begin to jump rope. She and he sit on the swings. The swings are bound to the iron frame by chained links, and they hold their weight without difficulty.

When they get off the swings, they entwine their arms around one another's neck. They are not looking at one another. They do not question what this move may signify. They are enjoined without sight of what thrust to which future. Come along, see the impediments. The words come now mostly in her head. She is worried about being found out. She is worried about the monster. The monster, strangely enough, appears to her with a ribbon around its neck, with a bow in front, to the side. It is a deep rich pink, this ribbon.

The monster bows to her.

She thinks of all the male egos she has stroked, pacified, in order to be included.

She and he take their arms back to themselves.

He wants a run; he wants to gallop. He wants them to run alongside one another. He doesn't know how to tell her this.

She tells him that their love perhaps could calm their individual monsters. He asks: But could our love heal them?

Our love has to meet and know and work through the monster, she says, and that, you are right, means going through a lot of power destructive motions which only can be restored by the Love that is beyond history.

Are not our monsters beyond history? His question is sincere.

Yes, in the sense that they move through our families over and over, but not beyond history entirely like Love. Love is what lets us endure the monster repetition and the overwhelming, out-of-control expression of that as it emerges in one or the other or both at the same time. Over and over emerging without putting us under. This Love is not human yet the embodiment of who knows us from before birth.

This Love is to become aware of monster which precludes projecting it and blame and curse which is to suffer it. Aware of it is the service of Love through continued prayer, felt and embodied repentance, abiding grace through suffering, allowing us to see to be aware of the monster's many parts, thus our own. Love including crucifying Love.

He wipes something off her cheek. She realizes the intimacy in the gesture. She realizes that the monster is breathing more evenly now.

They want to find a hearth fire and wrap up at its base. They want to go further than the sipping of cocoa, beyond the soapy bath, beyond the steamy soup. They want the basic, gray, wool blankets; not even plaid is necessary now.

They want to wrap up there, together as alone but not the sort of loneliness which cavern housed monster.

Yet it is too early in their interchange for wool blanket intimacy. So, they are continuing on the walk. They are avoiding the black ice. They orient to their field of vision. There are no hearths in sight. She begins to feel the sob come. She begins to wonder on this relation of monster to the greater Love beyond history. Does it need their love to get there?

Is the monster dependent on us? She asks him. She feels like crying, she is tearing up. Or, she continues, is it all blah blah, are we going nowhere?

He surmises: All of the monsters do need us to change so they can want to.

Why is that such an incredibly sad thought, she wonders aloud and continues: I guess it's because we do not know that need of the monster, or even that we have a monster, so we get possessed and act it all out, so it just become our magnified need, charging, desperate and so the monster fragments into its many parts. Each of our engagements with significant others in our lives brings out a different part of it.

Like, she adds: 2-year-old wanting all of it. Leader and all must be on one's own side or humiliated and strikes out either blatantly or through the pen or sharp tongue if not. Or older and feeling oneself royalty wanting utmost respect and subservience. Intelligence spurning the stupidity around it. Manipulator hiding within the goodness to get what it only feels it can get by manipulating for its own security. And that's just a few. All are variations of Reed, Brocklehurst, and Rochester.[54] He has read it, he understands.

It's like a churning butter sound, he replies.

Without the fruit of it. Why butter? she asks.

Came to mind. We all just churn along, I suppose, while monster is out there, dangling in caverns, ever lonely and ever threatening. But it hurts, it wants too much. It ravishes.

I'm hungry, he adds. I cook a simple supper, she replied.

Time exchanges. They switched watches, and then switched them back again. She sang the opera in her head or rather let it sing there. As if it were enclosed. As if it were enclosed and not trying to bite itself out.

She goes about her house duties; she trips over an extension wire. She had meant to push that into the line where wall met floor. She had meant for it to be part of that meeting: a third interjected in the meeting of the other two without compromise or intrusion. She had meant it, but it never happened and then she tripped.

The thirds. We do look for them, she thought, even when they are not explicitly provided.

---

[54] See essay at the beginning of this book.

She ironed the handkerchief in a precise triangle. She thought of the enlarged crawl space that had come in the dream. Compared to the one in the house of her upbringing, the dream crawl space not only had been extended and heightened, yet also had many compartments. One could walk upright beneath the entire house in the dream crawl space, which was almost empty, cleared out, except for a few boys with a TV, way back into it.

What do they want? What do they need? She was wondering while ironing. About 16 or 17 years old. When she thought about how much had been cleared out in the dream crawl space, she was relieved, but there were the boys, the TV.

TV relaxes the mind or can to do depending on the show, on what shows.

She eased into the dream memory as she ironed.

The hiss from the steam engineered from hot metal to linen. The hiss not angry or thwarted. The hiss so comforting in fact. It was the hiss of a cat wanting a bit of a release and actually being fine, not even perturbed.

When she got to the lace trim, she lowered the heat.

He was knocking on her door. She could tell it was him by the rhythm and the care. It said: let me in please but I will live fine if you cannot; though I prefer to be in, not being let in will not cut my breath off and yet I breathe more perfectly when with you.

This was another sort of opera. Call it post-modern, call it harmonic until the age is named since all creative flux eventually settles for categorization.

She called out his name followed by: come in.

Enter. Sons of so many categories. There were a few still in her crawl space now more basement. He didn't want to be one of those. His demeanor said so when he came in. She wanted to rest with him. She knew that his entry, when she was in the dream crawl space seeing those boys signified that the boys were between them, a third, and what still had to be lived and grown. She took the plug out of the socket and the iron hissed more loudly then as if a final exasperated call saying so am I done yet?

The remorse within her monster was lifting, she felt it the more she was with the one who knocked and entered: less impulse to tell him what was wrong, less hiding the aggression that did come up because of what was wrong, fewer eruptions.

But as the monster quieted and became more teenage boys lulling themselves and contriving, the other parts were still there: call them archetypes – hero/heroine, trickster, rebel, fool, mother, maiden lover, knight, monk, wise woman, so many, maybe countless.

They were in their own circulation with one another and with him. His figures corresponded enough with hers, as did his monster with hers, that they could meet and be in this circuit. But the monster in each was part of how the parts divided. That roar from which each part attempted to pacify, relate, or forget.

She knew it when she and he were in their "upper register" – where they would go when most frightened, the place of remembered and reenacted punishments, or tortures, and so they each went high above to be compatible or to manipulate. Even their voices went up.

When the monster got upset, as it would, as they reenacted the older wounds and power plays with one another, then their voices were more the lower combined with high registers, the venom of the mind with the force of the appetite and libido. Power entanglements and roughness. Then there was less consciousness within and behind what was said and felt.

Today both their voices were more in the middle heart register, more authentic, more conscious, questioning, open, and safe.

So he came in when she was ironing. The hissing eased out. He put out both hands and she walked out behind the ironing board and extended hers. The touch of his hand was supple, unintrusive, and fully dyadic. He led her to the couch. Love seat or merely an appeal to appetite; appetite for love as per custom disguised as appetite for sexual bind.

Would she have preferred to dance in the space beyond the ironing? Does she feel a threat of entanglement? What intellectual contortions can she rely upon now? How to stay in the middle registers when the upper and lower need protections? The fathers got confused in the move to earth and the move to womb within earth. And they fled. The knight armor was taken up by women as it got rusty.

No ant could survive in this metal. It was not bugged. It got the job done. These women were tough. But the competition spirit, needed to put on the knight armor to begin with, was tearing their femaleness off since it had gone on too long in the withdrawal of the men.

Her tears were slow. Almost imperceptible to him as searing beneath lash. One, two… a space where another shirt sleeve carefully could be ironed, three…, the back of the shirt and its front could be ironed, four…

He was about to put his left arm around her when he noticed the tear. It was more like he smelled it. It was like some sweet scent coming from the kitchen even long after the cookies were taken out of the oven and off the sheet.

He followed the scent to her eye, to beneath it. Her eyes looked straight ahead. They only blinked once the entire time he was looking at them. And it was that blink that prompted more tears to run down, as if scurrying after one another. No plops just a simple regard for a space of rhythm where nothing was possible of getting ironed out.

He took his left arm away from moving to her back and took her right hand in his left. More tears followed this contact, and some found the way to his knuckle.

His stomach ached, it felt like the punch that never came could come at any second.

She realized at that moment the level of her exhaustion. All gloves came off and were put by the side of the knight armor that had been placed on the floor, creaking its way to rest.

Her heart in the mid chest was crying.

His stomach ached.

Her tears were ceasing. The body knows to come up in the water. The breathing evened though not in synch yet with his which still was almost rapid.

The elaborately wrapped gifts that forgot why they were so dressed up.

When her stomach began to ache, she looked at him. He was looking down and seeing nothing. The gray in front of him was comforting and sustaining.

If she acted first, she would be the earth father or sky mother. None of that was called for here.

Her stomach ached more. She longed for a cheery pie, the break into the tart skin to the pleasurable goo that welcomed the chewy cooked dough.

She focused on that pie on order not to be earth father or sky mother. She then saw that she could take the reins and some horse she must know, of which she must be intimately familiar, would carry her away.

To take or not to take those reins. To rein in or on, to persist in refusing to use the knight armor to protect from the debris from an atomic blast decades ago still finding its way back to them. But she did not want that armor to further rust and become decrepit in its corner either. It had served its purpose when bodies were the weapon. Then came the gunpowder, then atomic smoke, now words from eon sources of hate finding its way through. No metal could guard now. She let the armor go.

How to sit on the aka love seat after the tears, after the stomach eased in both of them? How to know the words of hate coursing through their histories, their family's hardened palms, ancient and current? How to know the words enough so they do not have to be fired out? These were the words in the tears, and he began to hear them now. Their monsters met and were dissolving in the tear.

She turned to him and told him that after all she did not want to leave him. She let the horse out into the pasture to its delight.

She told him that they could put their respective, inherited, abusive and overused words of hate on a wall, in many frames.

Would we then lock up the room? He asked it carefully. He was trying to sort through what she was saying without judgment or concern.

That might defeat its purpose, no? Don't we have to refer to them often as we feel them rip through and try to claim us, to tear us within as apart from one another? Don't you feel their pull now? They want to tear us from this loveseat. They want us to ride off in different sunsets.

So we'll frame them and put them in scrapbooks like of old.

He put his left arm over her shoulders. They sat together quietly for many minutes. She thought of the cartoons she would watch as a child. Distraction or cure? There was an uncertainty of a certain pleasure there. Yet there was no place for humor here.

Or was there?

She looked at him. She plucked his cheek. A gesture of fondness. Of familiarity. None of them can reach us here now at this moment, she said. It's between the two of us.

And those framed words of hate? He added it cautiously.

Collecting and placing them in scrapbook is why we can make sure others do not magnify them in our lives to destroy our union.

He said: I know it's not enough to say Love is what allows us to keep them for view but not go under them.

But Love is in the framing and placing them, isn't it? Isn't that what made the frames? Made the process of putting them in the book so we can study and know them, so we are not static in those entrails?

Yes, he agreed, all of that.

And the music surrounding and running through and circulating between the frames - is not that Love?

Yes, that too.

And then they went out. The sun was almost too bright as if the broad rays were spotlighting their union. The sun has no desire, she whispered to his left ear. It wore itself out in the carnival last year. It had the wide leg-raising dance with the country girls there and it got exhausted. Then days of rain and wind.

The thin gold necklace he placed on her neck was fitting beside the gray pearls. He continued: the sun had left each country girl with a necklace around her neck. The way her mind would now engage the throat to speak her mind and her desire. Dancing with the sun is no joke.

Which of us is the sun? She asked it directly.

Or are we both one figure dancing with it? He asked back.

What do we want from it? What does it want from us? How to tell the difference?

To be one figure in the eyes of the sun is not to be fused. He said it clearly yet almost as a question.

Do you worry about that? she asked timidly.

I worry about everything, he responded.

The sun wants to relax us into our union. It is not dismayed. It does not want to sabotage us with fusion.

This question of desire again and again.

The force of it pushing through.

And isn't it time we asked what it wants? It's never completely ours, that force of desire.

The apple blossom tree is ripe and poignant for only two weeks. But its glory remains flowing in the fallen petals that stay on the lawn long afterwards. And even when they dry almost to a crumbling, the glory is there.

Feeding the lawn?

In the crumbling, in the desiccated slivered rose fibers.

They went over to a tree standing in a lawn by the road. They examined its roots. What it wants is no crime. What it wants is rosy without escape from remorse or melancholy inclusive of repentance. What it wants is for us to touch these roots half in and half out of the ground. Old, reaching, tremulous when spoken to tenderly and not off handed.

What it wants is for us to see that these roots are of the best for all of us. Our common regard of what levels us. The excrement in the morning, the last thought before falling asleep, the piece of crusty bread caught in our teeth.

What it wants is the appeal of the puppy in our arms. The yapping ceases when we look in its eyes and hug it further. What it wants is for us to know how the baby too relaxes almost to a complete smile when we see into its eyes and recognize who it is. What it wants is the din in our inner canals to ease and calm.

It wants the end of skin diseases and kidney failures. It wants the repose that is ignorant of and not needing artificials. What the sun wants, after all, and what these roots want are in synchrony.

The broad rays of the sun seemed to have a rose lining and the two were not wearing glasses. A true rose. A message from the patroness of small things being worthy and even sacred.

Rose lined sun ray, broad ray, ignite our being together, our finding of this valve opening to discarded black clog carrion of undigested relationships now digest together the meal sunbaked finally.

The nephew rejoices. The nephew bounds. They are visiting together. It is the first time they as a non-fused couple or individual make the visit. The visit was made sparingly. The tear stain on her cheek when the couple had been sitting side by side was still felt and heard. It was a drier ridge. It did not bode happenstance but was not greedy either. She was not crying her days away. Nor was she trying to rest alone on the love seat, passive, open, and dismayed.

The nephew was bounding. His heart always had pumped faster than the others, even as his demeanor was evenly paced. His smile could inform either ear, he was a happy young man. Even when walking, he stepped off the balls of his feet in memory of bound.

When she cried that night, the tears were more peaceful, they were limited and resourceful.

He just placed his left palm on her upper back. He had the thin gold chain she had given him on that wrist. What he heard in her tears resonated with his own. After they had sat and then taken the walk, he took off the gold insignia ring from his pinky finger on his right hand. It would stay in the jewelry box until a later inheritance.

Someone was pulling a trigger. Someone was enjoying spying on them and wanting to destroy the connection. He had on a dark sweatshirt with a hood that was on over his head. But then she saw him out of the corner of her eye and realized that he was in the mist and from an ancient past. She told her loved one and they focused on the gold wrist chain and the thin gold necklace that fitted well with her gray pearls. They stared upon these circles. They let the gold be. They let the gold assort the ancient past which must return, cyclically, until it spends itself through prayer for the wider Love.

For they had heard in their sobs: prayer is no laughing matter. Prayer is crucial in this spending. Prayer is the links in the gold. The mist surrounding the dark sweatshirt man says: the gold is bestowed on us, but we have to work to get to it.

It is not about false hopes, she whispers. It is uncanny how we wish without supplicating. It is uncanny how the confessional is possible.

He touched her earring. He wondered what she had heard. They remembered together the beach ball and playing on the beach. The encapsulated wonders. The searches. The tie-dyed tank tops. The rounded calves and tightened buttocks. The toughened soles and the sandy toenails, sand between toes. Interlocking memories.

They refused to get toe rings. That was too much.

They supped with the nephew and his new family. They engaged in more frivolity. They lit the candles. They sang the songs almost hymns now as the hour moved past midnight. They clasped hands and the sweat between them was happy, no need of poignancy. Not regretful or making up for lost time, yet totally grateful and ensured. Rest assured of my prayers, she always had said.

All slept well under various ordained ceilings. The sobs rested in her chest. They were not over but having been heard they knew their place. They did not carry disease anymore and she was no longer frightened of germ.

The next day they said temporary goodbyes and when the couples were waving, they all thought that they heard Christmas bells. The stalking hooded man was over. The hooded man had become part of the family.

Share the tide. Sharing the tide. No frame seems possible around it yet there is the shore, there is the horizon. Here would be something else to frame. They smell the tepid salted air, the air with a hint of the pulse of the snail's beat. They share the salty hotdog covered with sauerkraut. The crisp carbonated drink to supplant salt. The gulls calling from the base of their throats, the longing that approaches every tide. They walk along the edge of the water. He prefers the dampened beach sand, she the hot sand, and the line between the two is running below their clasped hands.

She is smiling. Her eyes greet other beach walkers. The look gazes welcome and move on. Walking motion along the energetic tide. Does it not ever tire? She is asking him; she is asking it. She is feeling its pull in her groins. She wants to shake it out. She does not want to hear it or feel it again.

She imagines swimming in the indoor pool. It is long. She makes it to the other end, yet she is very much out of breath. She holds onto the cement ledge and breathes deeply. Breathes heavily. Breathes speedily. She realizes that he is the right mate for her because he does not dive in to save her mid lap nor does he have investment in the strokes, in the passage which ultimately and fervently is her own; yet he watches from the edge.

Cement frame or shore horizon frame. Which to prefer? They are different in this way, this preference of what frames their water. Essentially, he says, the frame relates to the source of the water. Which source is preferable? Rhythmic moon or water tank hose? How human does each of us want to be when beside the water or within it?

How, she adds, do we know ourselves human when buttressed and rolled by tide, when we dare to peer when beneath and face the sea creature, the one who has not a care in the world and does not need to know us at all, may not even want that? I will be less afraid of the pull of the ocean tide now.

I remember, he tells her, taking an exam once. We had our separate desks and only pen and paper. The questions were evenly aligned. The questions were fair. There was a certain transference to the teacher that made doing well possible and desired. I sat there with my ankles crossed beneath the desk. I had my head in the hand that was not writing. I was imagining that I was dreaming, that I was in the dream as I wrote out the test. It seemed like already there had been so many of them, these tests, and I knew there would be so many more, that this dream would continue dreaming. I think your question and my question on what frames the water, what its source, are on another test.

Who is the teacher then? She asks with a smile and then says: that is the obvious question. I know the teacher goes to Church. I know the teacher encourages others to go to Church. I know that even this walk this talk, every word may be part of the tests. But there is not judgment as much as consequence. The consequences of each thought and word and how we communicate is the grade, so to speak.

They are swinging their clasped hands now in the beat of their synchronized steps. They each hear a different nursery song in the spritely step.

There is the long song still in the atmosphere that rises about the nursery ones, and, when the couple orient to it, they hear the gulls, the sea creatures, the mollusk in the dampened earth as well as her wet palm reaching to and grabbing the permanent cement ledge as she gasps for air.

Everything is a competition. Even for those most holy, it's hard to avoid. She had been thinking that as they were sitting in the Church pews after Mass and now as they are walking out into the sun shining with less slant. They were incarnating doctrine in the way they were asked to live it in life called reality aka.

They usually favored the shorter path home, but they were not ready to sit at home. They may have been looking for a dog to absorb the daily structures. And more: to experience the Love in doctrine in skin and fur and wet nose contact. Some dogs had fur, some hair. She was not going to be allergic to her dog. She wants the full embrace, unencumbered, fulfilled. She wants to put a collar on it that says ownership, care, and where to go in case of an emergency.

They understood the weight of it: this going the long way to find their animal. Scouring the papers and screening the ads though educative were not helpful.

She rested her head on his shoulder as he drove. The pastures passed reminiscent of Scottish growth and fecundity. It would not be that sort of dog, however, not British this time, large, bounding, and focused. Though they each had an abundance of care capacity, they did not have the energy for large dog bounding need for exercise; they were aging in approaching mid-life. A mid-sized dog, more mellow, would do.

The time of the movies is over. They said goodbye with little fanfare. Some goodbyes take drums and timbals. Some timbals have a thin purple lining the circumference. When they are hit, they generate other hues depending on the tone. When the goodbye is due or overdue, then the hues complement the purple. When the goodbye is catastrophic, they sour it.

Goodbye to the cinema, going into the large dark room with strangers to level oneself in group affect, well that passed. Call it germ warfare. Call it the rudeness of others not brought up with social manner, and hurt so much, lacking basic security, with a pain yet unrecognized so their behavior in crowds was self-aggrandizing and often too loud. So the movies passed away.

She thought how he and she were shooting their own films. Daily. Hourly. She thought of riding another sort of horse and letting it go its own way. She thought of how he would be filming that somewhere and that assured her, leaning to the flank, that neither she nor the animal would get carried away.

She checked her watch. The diamond was tiny in the center where the two hands intersected. It was a gift from her father this diamond though she was not sure how it ended up in the watch. The diamond also was where their hands intersected, when they were in Church and now in the great design of the pastures, looking for a dog they could call their own: a dog they might call Spot or Mike but most likely the name that emerged when the eyes of this potential interlocked with theirs. The diamond would be at the midpoint of that too.

Yet no dog yet. The sadness descended before the night even began to fall. She thought it had just descended in her circle but then she saw the curvature of his mouth and knew it had come to visit them both.

It was like carrying their child who had fallen asleep, back to its bed. It said: forget the pastures for now. They will not go away like the movies, they stay. It is time to go home. Your new dog is there. Just look behind the couch. Push the couch away from the heat unit and see what is laying there for warmth and comfort.

The dog was there, and it was listening in its sleep to the gentle words of the early Medieval monk from long ago. The words were about the Lazarus who lived again, so that is what they called him.

The talk of the town. The hearts generate like a train engine its coal. The gyration somehow emanates and catches onto the whirr of other hearts, like a contagion or pulses replicating in the air. Get back to yourself. This is what they most likely were conveying. Get back to yourself. Remember that all is well even with sin prevalent all will be well, and grace is everywhere. Take that in the everyday plodding step by step. Make the scones for Christmas. Rejoice in the new naked babe at Easter. It is all good, remember even as the gyrations disturbing heart remind turmoil and not being sufficiently greased.

The weight of the wheels crunches the earth but does not mine it. The wheels have ridges encased in the dirt that would prefer being on the pasture yet establishes itself in its lot.

She took the reins. They were on the front of the wagon and their dog was between the two of them. They had borrowed the wagon to take their bundles to the next town. He wanted her to learn how to drive it. The horses were new to them yet readily responded to their touch and click. Click click tongue in cheek yet the horses knew to pick it up. They knew that the horses really knew the way and just went along with the click click.

If we each could know our slot. It takes generations to know. Click click. The diamond between our hands holding each other sometimes falls away and we do not even notice until much later. Telling the truth helps remember that it is gone. Then we look beneath the stove, under the couch, in the back of the rear drawer, but to no avail. It feels like suffering, it feels a weight and an absence both at the same time.

Sometimes she would have to say something twice to be heard. It was as if something slashed the end of her heart, upper quadrant. Gyrations disturbing heart. What holds, what can support such? We try to go backwards, she told him as she was steering the wagon with the reins and click click. We try to go back but then we can get stuck and die for the mother. To be enwombed. She wanted to put her head on his shoulder like she does when they are in the car or train. But she had the reins now, she had to sit straight. She was finding her slot and the word was that the diamond would be there.

They had sodas at the corner store. Soda pops. They clicked their bottles together as if it was the stronger hops beverage. No slant, no slur, no surge intended. We each go our own way into our slots but then they start speaking with one another, for the slots have their own voice and cadence. The slots know the way. And when the danger comes, they choose not to ignite yet recede and wait.

This patience comes at a cost. It wearies the heart, but it is not the pain of those gyrations reminding turmoil and not being sufficiently greased.

The roads were packed down long ago yet this one not so much, and the dirt, remembering its olden time in pasture, is in the wheel ridge. Ridge roads to the high plains to amity and beaver creeks to new hampshires. The rest is in synchrony, but it never feels that way at the time.

Know yourself. Know your slot. The most difficult lesson. It is fine to get an F and keep trying. Others come and go. They become the search. Purpose runs through it like a thread of a whispering river whispering do not go yet, stay and pick up the thread, it is all clue. It is always what will be left when the others go to sleep.

The expense of the dawn. Once he had named her fawn and she sees them at times now with their deer. After the ravages of the gyrations, the war-torn heart piecing itself back, the deer can return to being fawn again yet safe.

The tidy room satisfied. She had decorated it for holiday, for mirth, for the ever-engendered compass of lights. The stuffed animal in the corner shelf mimicked their dog in color and attitude. Once she thought she had bought it for others' children, but then saw it insignia. How to lower to the seriousness of it, the plights, the disagreement, and cracked cement on the side of the building, on the sidewalk. Hire the plumber and do not be dismayed at the price. The terrible two's. The one who has given up crawling.

Summary of affairs. They are throwing an orange between the two of them. Game as well as reminiscence. Her leather sandals did not allow the full jump and leaping for it, catch the orange, but sufficed. Back and forth until it ripened and should either get thrown out or eaten immediately.

Her neck ached in the back, in the sinews so tired of carrying the head to body and back and forth. No orange this but stemming from it. Orange as root. And the growth body to head and back; the neck is exhausted. The neck sings out. Holy Angels of High please incarnate and touch this sinew too long a passage of what conflicts, what never knows how it got to be in the twin bed.

The sauce was cooking on the stove, and she made sure to keep stirring it so it would not burn on the bottom. No rough browned residue of the temperature out of synchrony, not allowing the spread of molecules embrace to the unscorched taste, not disregarded, or say the neglect is as bad as abuse. Just everyone providing for oneself since that was already too much. So she stirred the sauce and it flowed without lump or scorch. It covered what used to roost. She was considering more a plant diet.

The yarn felt softly stimulating as she moved it between her fingers. Fingers seldom get the stimulation since they are so busy giving it. It is the inside skin, that which lives between them, along the inside of each, that really longs for it, the touch from outside. This desire is so little noted or represented even in the best of text.

Waiting and the Prince did not disappoint. She had been looking in the wrong directions because her neck sinews were not communicating due to the ache.

Even with sin prevalent, all will be well, eventually. It is just about the wait and not taking matters in one's own hands to stimulate prematurely. That never satisfies the inside side of each finger, anyway.

The dog with the collar was barking. The dog, theirs, was bounding outside. It no longer, finally, was about the orange passed back and forth or the badminton. Air borne all eventually falls. Monotonous urgent attempts to keep it lifted. Please, mother, father, do not fall for or evade your continual wish to avoid the hole of death that is rightly yours. All the running about. All the glitter.

Call the cousins. Engage histories that have fallen away and no longer will ignite. Ashes stirred and that has a grin over it. Transparent and of care though long past.

Holidays. Once it had been what appeared scrumptious feast but doused always doused. And that alcohol would ignite often so now in memory those ashes finally are cold, are not harried or wanting revival.

Very slowly her shoulders let down or begin to do so. Very slowly she feels those muscles stop such brace. She does not have to brace their disability any longer. She can let the stumble happen on its own accord. That is the holiday spirit. That is the broad smile that goes across her heart, and she is certain others feel it too.

They sat at the curb. They were tired of choosing bends in the road. They each had a chill yet felt it differently. She chewed what be chewing tobacco in the past yet here was a very tasty leaf chosen carefully with gentle pull off the berry bush. No poison this time. She pretended to notice the many others so they would not feel abandoned.

She coaxed the leaf off and then took it in her mouth after offering it to him. But he was trying to clean out of leaves. He was waiting for the spices of the season. Whoever knows what we feel, the most mysterious function of all. Whoever knows yet here is something that cannot be patented.

'Don't rip it that way.' Was it a second-grade teacher? The third grade one was benevolent and would have said it differently; she was soft-spoken and old in her young years, Greek. Strange, she thought and then said it to him, who nodded as she spoke, we only remember the names of the ones who were really kind or those really not. Yet even memory is less mysterious than feeling.

The effort to cook. Most use wine to get through. She did not drink; he had given it up long ago. Longing was toying with them on occasion, but more like ribbon candy floating through the air and they were not caught and did not catch it, that drift.

She looked up – no balloons, no cotton candy, no ribbon candy, no fireballs that made one's tongue pleasurably burn. The sweetness that followed was bland in comparison with the first hit of burn. She did not burn the dinner often, hardly at all.

It got cold out. They cuddled with one another on the curb. They heard the Christmas bells from afar. Then the bells got louder – like the police car siren getting louder as closer when one realizes that it wants to get by, pull over, it's an emergency. The exhaustion after wrapping all the gifts. Yet it always is Christmas.

And what if there was a small puddle at this curb that we hardly could see? She asked him, continuing: what if our feet are getting cold from that puddle and that's why the chill? He wrapped his arm around her more surely. No, she added: our socks are thick and guard us from such hidden puddle. The rebel in us will thicken the sole of our heel.

They missed their dog Lazarus, so they decided to walk back. The Christmas bells would alternate loudness as they rounded the bends. By the time they entered their home, the sound was in the home, and they slept well that night, Lazarus cozy by them; it went into the walls, each and every one, and became an insulation.

She had been crawled up in the corner of the crawl space in her second dream. She rose then in spirit, past the rebel boys and their TV, past the mentor/seducer with the high bookshelves and ladder posed and ready. She rose with the ribbon around her neck tied with a fancy knot, red and tinged with magenta. Who owns her now? she wondered. So many definitions of freedom and worth. Is worth contingent upon feeling? She still was rising. She took the wood fragment out of her left triceps. Some days she went the whole day forgetting it was there, but today, in the rising, she remembered.

She would be the tasty bread, finally ready to come out of the oven, she would eventually slow to it. Now she had been given the ticket in Spirit, God ordained. She was cooked enough. She descended having no idea where or how she would land.

And where was he in it all? She looked around. The horizons seemed endless. The sound in her ear thwarted. She had been talking for decades in evasion and knowledge. The knives were taken out of the quiet. She earned it. Sweat and tears they used to call it.

When the animals came running, rushing really, from the horizons towards her. She suspected safari animals, but they were domestic and just very hungry. She licked her own lips as she was descending. Where was he after all?

The mind keeps going. This bread will have a clear mind yet all kneaded. The smell so alluring, appealing like the Christmas bell so the sound in her ear discharged itself. When she landed, she could hear again.

The animals ran towards her. This is when she realized she was in the second dream so went back into it, unafraid and unassuming. The animals ran towards her. She felt some power leaving her. They all were so hungry – would they attack? Where was he? Who would protect or whom would she protect in order to be protected? Then, shockingly, the animals skidded to a stop before her. There was enough bread for each of them and she was not eaten or even bit at.

She awoke still in the corner of the crawl space. The boys had come in from their own band rehearsal. They were drinking beer; there was something random on the TV. One of them was shy and came stealthily over to her with a small bouquet of flowers. She wondered where she could get a vase down here. He offered them to her without saying a word. This was the sort of exchange that was to be the way from now on.

The talk of the mind would knock on her door, would ask her to run from choosing death, would warn her about their words. But it was to be in the bread now. It was all in the time and what ordained outside of it. Perfect pitch she had written once. Perfect pitch in perfect time. Yet the fear of this exchange tempted her to call upon easy contrivances, the old gods.

She stood up and walked out of the crawl space. The boys followed her, they were hungry too and it was the time for their rise to the upper stories. And for this she had to be more of the bread.

She went up and went to sleep. On the brass bed that used to spend the envy, but now was discarded, forgotten yet still possible to sleep on and to wake finally to live out the dream.

Do not enhance the contrast through a megaphone. When she woke, he was there. Heat and burn it. They used to say the entrails were burning now it was a switch for the better. The little dog Lazarus had the ribbon on his neck that had been once on hers. They all were in the kitchen together. The baking was complete.

The furry thing had not been in the crowd of domestic, fervently hungry animals in her dream. The past was knocking in their heads like an automatic hammer. They looked at one another questioning how to stop it, how to pull that switch. Lazarus was snoring in his pillow bed now. The children have come and gone. The gifts have been delivered. The fairy godmother's kisses blew high where others lived. She was no longer divorced. She kissed goodbye the screen that the frenzied other dog once had charged through when that family was deteriorating, frayed, kept, and pounced upon by the memories of members long dead and dust.

Lazarus was sleeping in his pillow bed and snoring slightly. The hammers ceased. She had landed. She was of the bread. Where was he when she was of the bread? In the chambers. In the cabinets there. Waiting. Waiting in due time for her to knock and slip the handle back so he could come through and know the safety is not pine or mahogany, cedar, or oak.

When he was outside the cabinets, he looked her over as if for the first time. She smiled and he saw a bit of chocolate on her upper lip. He licked his finger and then wiped it off. She knew the lessons. She had been the conscientious student though she never lorded it. She said to him: how can I be the queen when I have the chocolate lipped? He said: it is to be something else. The fairy godmothers are gone and

so are the thrones. They went the way of the knights. They
went when you were having your dream placing the rebels
and learning how to descend as of bread.

The peacefulness of the sidetrack. Its curbs are jostled yet
unafraid. She heard him say that he almost heard the
megaphone. He was glad he was out of the cabinets, and he
described to her how she had descended into being of bread
with mind a main ingredient, not completely tangential at
all. The rest was spices and the specific exact type of non-
instant flour.

Kneading enough. Kneading granted enough. She was
not worried, and when the fear in her stomach came, well
she was not perplexed or in denial yet went there as the right
flour, as the minding ingredient.

Whose birthday would it be this day of so much
fragrance? They walked along the curb of the sidetrack. The
curb had regained its composure, and the sidetrack was
relieved. They lived through the moment together. He after
all held her in high regard. He wanted to stomp through the
woods, but stampedes were in her blood and she was for
decades seeking their release.

Let's walk gingerly. Let's sing the same tune in our heads.
Let's know our complements and see how we match. Then
we will take the personality test and see what springs forth –
like a loose screw, like a slinky. The temperaments will not
bind us for life. What passes through the diamond in our
hand holding is the rectification to this walk on the

recovered curb. They clapped their hands in synchrony. They released the record and it never mattered how or when it sold, for it was good.

She laid on the ground at one point and her tongue touched the earth. She was brown bread, and this came as a gentle surprise to both of them. The raisins were not there yet but on their way. The delay was forgiven and even a help.

When the train came, there was some ignition and she sat up. He reached for her hand and together they stood. Girls still hope for the rings on that finger. What's to prevent the trap? Secret wish engorged in throats afraid to swallow. Lazarus is the trap let loose. Lazarus love and the holy ground between them.

They waited for the train to pass. They had that mighty look between them. They buddied up together. They went through what forestalled. They saw go by the prim blouse with the peter pan collar just needs a circle pin on the right. The earrings could match but best be petite. Size of the hallow elephant looking out of the train car. Looking right at them whether registered or not. They fell into some familial rhythm with the train. They did miss it when it left to embrace one horizon. Each train is different and this one knew its way which now did not include them.

So they continued to walk along the curb. All her sobs necessary for ingredient in making her bread, and he heard them, he intuited those he could not hear though he did not consciously know that at the time. He heard all her sobs. He couldn't be there when the earlier ones had poured but they were part of these, it all ingredient.

Not to be soapy, not to be engendered. The train whistle fizzled away. The timer went off and then exhausted itself and the bread was made. This bread was hearty. It was enough for the main meal when that time came, when that time went.

They applauded together in the aftermath. The appeal sounded. They picked up their shoes and walked the rest of the way barefoot. Timely stepping. There was no crime here and the children were swinging their legs beneath their desks, all present at school.

She took off Lazarus' ribbon and put it away in her top drawer. She laid it beside the scissors which were not needed. The boy who came knocking on their window had grease in his hair, yet the wind still blew through it.

There was valentine in his hand. He just indicated it, he did not wave it or try to draw excess attention to it. She caught it in the corner of her eye and turned both eyes to it. The boy was smiling. The poet-rock star was still performing and so the heart was suspect. That drumbeat was in her canal and there was no getting around it. She turned both eyes to it.

He noticed, even from the distance of the window and behind the glass, that one of her eyes was slightly a different color from the other. There was a suggestion of green within the brown. So he had hope for her and he understood better why he had come. He lifted the valentine higher. He was very tempted to wave it, but he felt his own arm stalled.

What it must look like from the outside: a boy at the window holding up a valentine? For a moment, he stepped outside himself and saw how ludicrous that looked. Then he snapped back into place to be as completely present to her as possible. She came over to the window then.

The boy saw that the man with her had a diamond connection to her hand and this was there even when they were not in the vicinity of one another.

She came over to the window. The movement whetted her appetite. She wanted to eat it all up: the boy, the valentine, the way he attended to the green in her eye. But she waited. She stood there for what seemed like countless minutes. She waited until the drumbeat became very small and then left her canal. The poet-rock star was gone and that was it for her life, there would not be a return. She put her forefinger to the glass about where the valentine appeared through it.

She thought she heard someone lighting a cigarette, so she tried to rein in her focus. The boy probably can hear me through the window, she thought, but I will not speak. The man with her heard that and thought it was a good idea not to speak out loud.

She had taken the ribbon off Lazarus and the canopy over the bed went with it. The valentine was the red now. It was all the red that was needed. Because she had gotten to the bread, to be bread, she could endure it. The silence stood like a post.

Then she turned from the window, and it began to rain. The boy only took a minute of it and then he turned to go. The question of whether to make a last look, to turn around. To turn around is not to turn back. But it did not matter, the direction was clear, and he turned to go.

She thought of waving and did so in her heart which stopped suspecting. The time was over with the boy and the valentine. The yearning: be what I cannot get other where. That yearning will connect them though she could not.

When she turned from the window, there was green cast in her skin, not just in her eye. Is it the envy for all those who did not have to deal with that boy or the hope that in the space between them now something could configure that truly was good and at peace?

She went over to her husband and they ate. The time had come and gone, the time seemed to fly that evening. What it was like to sleep that night in the bed without canopy? There would be no silver on a tray brought to them in the morning. No silver. No tray. No willing servant. The valentine had gone.

The shock or dismay and those gossamer-like curtains did look somewhat frayed. She wiped the soup that had dripped on her skin. A small piece of pepper was there on the tissue. Green pepper, red pepper. The vegetable soup digested and full. The curtains could not fill in for the absence of the boy and so they were frayed.

She went over to them. She indicated to them that it was not their responsibility. She took them off the rod and she held them to her face now cleared of vegetable soup, now shiny and welcoming the fabric, even cherishing the soft regard of what would even try to fill in.

She snapped the elastic that she held in her right hand. She rubbed the curtain over her face and smiled. No forgiveness necessary. She could just let the curtain off the rod of its righteousness. It was not its responsibility. The pane had to be exposed after all.

Her energy was restored. She had gone limp, limpid, almost catatonic in motion when the boy's tracks were covered by rain, by leaves knowing no other direction. She had gone limp, but now, she held it to her in gratitude. She released it from its task, one that had been given through ages, seen as security necessity.

She released it from its task and folded it carefully. Should she put it in the back drawer or in the cabinet out of which her husband had come? She did not want to throw it out since then consciously or unconsciously she might buy another. She did not want to tarry in her day either. The writing was on the wall. She looked at it. She understood that what was there would also be in what and whom she encountered that day. She understood that the Author, who wrote, would be her life worth living. Author writing on blackboard and one can learn or not.

She is spending her life to know Author and living for that privilege. The Author who presents the precise echo of what written. For reasons she can spend a life ascertaining. She can fall on her knees in worship. It is enough, it is fine.

She folded the curtain very carefully; she did not want any hangnail or piece of rough skin to rip or tear it. There had been enough sorrow. The merchandise had been put away. She knew the file system of placement. So where to place this now folded curtain? She stoked her cheek with it one more time. There are so many levels of knowing which time is right, but then life gets seemingly rearranged and the writing on the wall blackboard says now.

She put the folded curtain in her drawer of dishtowels, those for everyday use and those for company. It can have a basic everyday life now and also be of special occasion without the huge responsibility to cover or fill in. Not that she would be so crass to use it for the dishes or her soapy, speckled hands. But it could rest in good company there.

There was so much to sort out and compile. It could rest there. It had once been the color of mint but now it more was of the dusty tired grass of late summer. She could almost see it multi-colored as she put it in the drawer. She could almost hear it sigh a sigh of relief, and it was calm, it was living in this new way, and it was calm.

She went over to him. He had been patiently doing his daily work at the table. He had taken the elastic from her right hand and put it on his right wrist to remind him to pick up the items on his errands: she should not have to stretch herself so dearly. The women in her literary history were happy. They went on with their silent applause. She thought of the child between them all: between her and him, between her and them. It was an unassuming child.

She remembered all who had departed inside and outside, and been commemorated, for this new one to begin to emerge. Soup is on. He said it in his heart, and she heard that. Soup is on. I have to go to find the baby, she replied. He said he could not yet hear a baby. It is in the far corner about 100 feet away, she said. That could be very far or very close, he said.

She felt the distance from those from whom the distance had come, had to be. She clutched at the dishtowel that she was using to wipe the counter. It was an ordinary one and it had not yet engaged with or even met the gossamer-like curtain drawered and safe.

She got out the soup bowls. This would be the left-over vegetable soup, yet it had aged well. Take off the apron. Were those words the wail? Was that what the baby wanted? She took off her apron. She was no longer apprentice. She put the dishtowel on its rack. This was not to be an affair of cleansing. This was not to be the blue iron rim of some enchanted evening either. She reoriented herself to the presence of the kitchen, of the soup heating, of his sorting through what errand.

Now do you hear it? she asked him. He looked up. There was slight film on his glasses. She saw through it. His look was dazed. Do you hear it? Again asking, almost a plea yet one with a certainty minus edge. He rubbed his eyes in order to hear better. He told her he heard the school bells. No, he corrected himself, school is over. The apron is folded and put away. The stars are bright this night.

Together they went outside and looked up for the shooting stars that had been forecast. He saw one but when she looked, it was gone. She went back inside, and he stayed out and saw two more. He came in to get her, but when she went out again, it was gone. She was in the no-sense of the departed and becoming stuck there. She could not hear the baby any longer. She went into the den and began unweaving some yarn. She cut some pieces and pasted them on the canvas. Then she colored around them in a way that made the yarn look like mounds of paint. She refined her search in the painting. She missed so many, it was beyond loss.

But then she heard the sound again now more like 10 feet away. She had a better sense of the baby within the wail. She felt its feet throw themselves out, back and forth, and then she heard the wail again. It implored her to remain. It told her of the birth canal. It told her how it had been rimmed in by the throes of those of the old country. She listened carefully. She told the baby to keep pushing out. The baby told her to keep pushing.

The stars that seem to be 100 million miles away or just reachable depending on the affairs of the heart. Do not align with the wrong men. Follow what gets prayerfully put in your silence when with others whether you understand that or not, whether you yet can read the writing on the blackboard. That was the teaching of the rim, that was the school lesson that was over. Either she had to follow it or not, but the engaged period of studying and ricocheting was over.

The flag announced it, and, yes, it was a sort of graduation. Alma Maters remain, and some even wear it on a finger, but the tense fibrous pull of the muscle does slack and over time there is the new birth.

Some babies come covered with the rim more than others and the rim permeates into their skin and it takes decades to work through if the parents had not a clue about such rim. Yet she had been to school for a long time and suffered it beyond hope.

The collar that now Lazarus was wearing was thin though comfortable. She took it off and washed it. She wondered at its pull, its hold. The holding, the mediation of what could this dog be thinking and how that coordinates with his paw.

She washed her dog and then she took a shower. The streams of spray on her back wove through to the taut fear. Babies take a lot of work. She picked up the soap and lathered. Babies come with a price and a long list of yet unheard sobs.

But school had defined her ears and they were rather sparkling. The shooting stars she could not see were wrapped around each ear. She heard the wailing again and this time put on her watch so she could stay attentive. It was not the one her parents had given her in hope that she would pull through the fervent suffering, but it reminded her of it, though this one did take the current time. It took and gave the time. Like the baby would.

So she dried herself off and got out of the bathroom smelling of the ocean in full tide high tide high time. She was no longer afraid of the ocean, she thought she was ready for the baby, though she trembled.

She trembled at the thought of moving forward but the creak in her hip could not take much more stasis and sitting in place. The time of the halt and study really was over. The Santa took off his beard yet kept on his glasses since those were his own. His teeth were his own too since he had cared for them from an early age, very carefully. His hands were weathered and seasoned well. He took off his rings before he held the children. He winked at her because he saw that she heard the wail.

Time slots whether we know it or not. She relaxed her hold on the steering wheel. She was trying to sit up straighter. Lazarus was on the couch with her, sleeping with his nose placed beside slightly beneath her thigh. He benefited from her smell. It soothed him to a gentle snore. He heard the wail, she was sure of it; he knew it was next and to be and he was fine with it, like a distant song that no longer needed instrumentation.

She marked off the irritants behind her forehead. They were enemies of the baby, certainly. She was ready for them in whatever shape or size they may appear. She stood ready even when couched, even when finally relaxing the steering wheel hold, so she could move, with his help, to the bed.

The pushing began again. Her wail became indistinguishable from that of the baby. She faced the baby who appeared in image before her. She noticed that her eyebrows were the similar shape of her own though the shape of the eyes more like his. She wondered what carrot would urge on the animal of this baby: what could I offer you to proceed to this basic, simple life of ours? No need mother. The words were shooting stars.

No need mother to regulate this birth. The canal warned of no silly interventions. The ink of the printer almost needed replacement. She captured the image of the baby in her mind's eye and put it in the drawer with the translucent curtain, behind and beneath the everyday dish towels.

She wanted to throw up her arms and scream the welcome, hear the discharge. It flooded her, this discharge. It was like walking or trying to walk in a nyc street during rush hour when each step felt like moving through natural mud rising to the knee, to the waist. Such a push for each step. And what would such mud want? To slow to it, to the baby required to pass through the canal rim and get what patterning would be life assignment unfolding, to apprehend and hopefully further transform.

Transitioning to another position and the dog Lazarus shifted too. Her connection with her dog was a part of the baby's coming to be, a sort of prerequisite. The openings in her body enlarged like the ear trumpets in olden days. She held the coarse cloth in her hands, wringing it as the baby decided the course. Lazarus woke and howled when the head emerged. That brought her loved one consciously back and he was holding them all. The baby recognized their smell, and the wail became more human sounding like 1 foot away.

A package was being opened and the tissue paper had sparkles on it. Its crinkling was the motion of the stars. The apple fell from the teacher's desk. A student picked it up expecting no reward. Gifts for bargaining were gone, were nugatory in this new baby coming through the rim of a canal long in motion, waiting, sure, conceived.

The bed spread the blood and neither he nor Lazarus were alarmed. The baby liked the wrapping in clean cotton. The baby liked being relieved of the mounds and wounds of oozing discharge. The umbilical cut and transpiring there enough air and the baby took to lying on her chest getting ready for breast, for a lifetime of gifts that were beyond bargaining, beyond the call of duty.

Now Lazarus howled again. She felt the call of wolves in it, and she was glad that they had taken him in since he had the loneliness of one removed from the pack in him, not alienated yet destined to be apart.

She let herself be swaddled in blankets that he had bought new and wrapped around her and baby. The heaviness of daily regard fell away. He prepared her a tasty meal of favorite food and drink. She dreamt, holding the baby closely, of new coveralls and all-weather boots.

Take the temperature and the baby was normal. It feasted on nutrients she long thought had left her but spontaneously appeared through her own skin. They were a close group now, four including their dog who now had his pack. They rearranged the furniture. The friends came in slowly and there was no risk of infection since they were hand-picked and the sort that knew and resisted the old germ warfare.

The tune of the season propelled them back to everyday routine. The canal of inner ear registered it and it played while she vacuumed the bedroom floor where all semblance of blood had been wiped. But she did not want to scour those boards. She wanted some scent to remain from the passage through that elemental canal. Do not take in too much of the ocean air, or too little, just breathe normally. Negative ions in woods and beach. Breathe normally. She vacuumed the kitchen and the living room as well.

The feeding was regular now and the soreness subsided. She was walking up the side cement stairs of the department store. She was looking for supplies for the new pack. All she wanted at the moment was a piece of gum, something to keep her from talking to wrong others, from the irrelevancies of the task. The stupefaction of the numbing days was over. It does not only come from hours of TV, she thought.

Yet relaxing only to the point of numbness, just to there and no further, was rich, would be orchestrated. All the tunes, and which hit. Which hit the mark and wonder how on earth could such a sound be. She could no longer conduct, the baby needed her, needed them. The tyranny of false obedience went its way. Simple regard took over. The cat in the alley of the store stared at her standing there holding the packages. The cat stared at her for a few seconds before skirting around the garbage cans, back to his companions of the night.

Then suddenly everything settled, and the scurrying cat and the alley remained a home for those who had stepped away from what could be called society, she was sure of it. She had once wanted to explore such alleys and, in fact, did. He had wanted no part of that which is why they could marry. The smells of those places did not distract her since the maps of her attic said others of her blood had been compelled to roam them, so must she have yet through grace had gotten by with the necessary perturbation.

Is it that the time is up or what is the function of will here in moving out of the alleys after the quota of suffering? Moving out of the alleys and the monster and its parts propelled through hate had been framed and were in their scrapbook. His monster aligned with hers, though his had come from places not the alleys.

She was in the lot finding her car. The bundle was light enough for this not to be a chore. The years of study, scrutiny of the books, the reading of the blackboard, the rearrangement of mental storages. To put those early explorers of the alley, those early transgressions when the tunes missed the mark, in the oven of her midriff and let them cook. Let them cook, as she kept at it, yes, will, through all the various alleys presented and in numbness sought after. Let it cook; finally, the teens emerged and were being fruitful.

Let them cook and then it becomes its own study and then it can help others. That is how the baby came when enough of that due paid in full.

She put the bundle of boxes in the trunk, and she went home. He was trying to make soup, but the baby needed more time than soup, than ingredients, than the sink holding what was sticky, coagulating. She took the baby after she unwrapped the outer wear and sat down taking off boots. He brought in the boxes and his nose penetrated slowly into them to examine what they contained. She kissed the baby all over. She put her right cheek to the baby's head stroking it so gently, it hardly was a touch; it could hardly break a record. But the tune did change as she did that.

It came out of the alley and oriented to lullaby. The map she had made of the alleys, while those drumming in her inner ear were now in the midriff oven, would last long enough. She held the baby up and looked into her eyes: we made the maps and now they sing. They sing as others can explore, without going under, they sing the direction, the symbol, the worth.

She took a gold coin, long disused, and touched it to her tongue and then she touched it to the baby's forehead. There was no wailing now. When the baby woke at 2 am, she and he both wake and, smiling at one another, hear the cry. Let this be the new gold of the depths superseding material gain or personal desire. What can that look like? she asks the baby, speaking it quietly in the tiny perfect ear.